ARE YOU LISTENING?

Takeaways

Are You Listening?, Lydia Sturton
Blue Fin, Colin Thiele
The Dog King, Paul Collins
Fries, Ken Catran
Get a Life, Krista Bell
The Grandfather Clock, Anthony Hill
The Great Ferret Race, Paul Collins
It's Time, Cassandra Klein, Karen Brooks
Jodie's Journey, Colin Thiele
The Keeper, Rosanne Hawke
Landslide, Colin Thiele
The Lyrebird's Tail, Susan Robinson
Monstered, Bernie Monagle
Mystery at Devon House, Cory Daniells
Ned's Kang-u-roo, Vashti Farrer
NIPS XI, Ruth Starke
Pannikin and Pinta & River Murray Mary, Colin Thiele
Read My Mind!, Krista Bell
The Rescue of Princess Athena, Kathryn England
Saving Saddler Street, Ruth Starke
The Sea Caves, Colin Thiele
Seashores and Shadows, Colin Thiele
Space Games, Mike Carter
Spy Babies, Ian Bone
Timmy, Colin Thiele
Twice Upon a Time, John Pinkney
Wendy's Whale, Colin Thiele
The Worst Year of My Life, Katherine Goode

ARE YOU LISTENING?

Lydia Sturton

Lothian
B O O K S

*For Danika, who doesn't often listen
but always says the right thing.*

Acknowledgement

The author would like to thank the Australian Society
of Authors for the mentor programme, and Gary Crew
for his enthusiasm and encouragement.

Thomas C. Lothian Pty Ltd
11 Munro Street, Port Melbourne, Victoria 3207
www.lothian.com.au

National Library of Australia
Cataloguing-in-publication data:

Sturton, Lydia.
Are you listening?

ISBN 0 7344 0198 1.

I. Title.

A823.3

Cover and text illustrations by Geoff Kelly
Cover design by Sandra Nobes
Text design by Paulene Meyer
Printed in Australia by Griffin Press

1

A frantic dash for the bus is a part of my everyday routine. It doesn't matter how early I get up, whether I eat breakfast or have a shower, details make no difference. Deep down where it really counts, time is not my friend.

One particularly windy morning I ran down the street having unkind thoughts about Sharon, who's never in a hurry *and* has perfect hair. At that precise moment my own hair was mounting a well-organised attack: blocking my nose, clogging my mouth, winding around my neck and getting impossibly tangled in my lucky silver chain. It obviously planned to choke me — but I was definitely going to have the last word!

'The skinhead look has a lot going for it,' I muttered, still running.

This was going to be a great day. Missing the bus was certain detention, my backpack was jumping up and down like a headless chook and I was having a chat with my own hair! There's only two sorts of people who talk to their hair, out-of-work movie stars in television commercials and total idiots.

I collapsed next to my friends, Sharon and Rose. I hadn't missed the bus after all, and immediately the day seemed several shades brighter. I'd been right the first time, though; this had been the bad start to what was going to be an even worse day! The beginning of a nightmare.

'I thought I was going to have to run to school again,' I gasped, when I could talk.

'The bus is four and a half minutes late,' stated Sharon calmly, which is so like her. She's clever, well-organised, beautiful, and even manages to be nice. It makes you sick, but it's not really her fault.

Just then I ripped my pocket rather badly, extracting a hairbrush and a disgusting grey-and-purple scrunchie. Rose was horrified.

'Look, you've ruined your dress! Why are you always in a hurry, Nicky?'

Sometimes she talks just like her own mother, or mine for that matter! Sharon doesn't bother to question natural phenomena; gravity, El Niño, 'Nicky's Lateness Syndrome'. She's not into wasting energy.

Rose is totally different; loud, cheerful and always telling bad jokes. Pity she never remembers them properly. We've been best friends since preschool, despite her habit of asking dumb questions. I decided to answer this one.

'It must be part of my genetic material. In my DNA there's probably an entire chromosome that arrived later than all the others. You know how I've tried, but things always seem to happen.'

'True, strange things happen *around* you,' said Rose.

She remembered the day last week when

I'd been seriously late for school. A bunch of guinea fowl had nested in Dad's vegie bed. He's paranoid about his stupid vegetables, which are totally organic. I knew he'd freak if anything happened to them, so Nicky to the rescue! I'd have to say if you've never come across any guinea fowl you're definitely winning. They sure are smartly dressed, but the size of their heads is a bit of a giveaway. Ask yourself, can a pea think?

I begged them to go nicely, followed by not so nicely. I pleaded, jumped up and down, and got very red in the face. Then I lay down on what had been Dad's prizewinning vegetables, and cried. All of this made not the slightest difference. They just carried right on — eeck, screeck, eerk; scritch, scratch, charge — until some stray thought made them pack up camp and trail off down the road, searching for another garden to ruin.

Feral birds don't rate that high when getting a late note from our school office. Then I had to put up with my teacher's corny jokes for the rest of the day — humour is definitely not her strong point. Actually, it's a bit difficult to say what is. Even though her eyelashes are rather mangy she wears loads of mascara, her piercing green eyes see around corners, her bum wiggles when she walks, and her number one aim is to make my life hell.

Another strange thing happened a little while before the guinea-fowl experience. This weirdo rang every afternoon to sing me nursery rhymes. I didn't particularly mind; his versions were cool, but Mum totally freaked when she found out. She even had our number changed, a slight overreaction I'd say. The weirdo doesn't ring any more, and neither do any of my friends as I keep forgetting to give them our new number. That's how come I've spent a lot less time on the phone recently, and a lot more time doing homework, a plus I suppose — schoolwork and me not being exactly compatible.

But it was definitely not my fault when the inflatable globe we use in class exploded in my face recently. How could it have been? I wasn't even touching it. I seem to attract blame for some reason. I didn't even get to finish my mapping assignment, so there was definitely nothing in it for me.

Things just happen when I'm around, it's not as if I ask them to, they just do.

Nothing like this happens to Sharon. I have this theory that tidy people are calmer because they don't allow any room for the unexpected. To tell you the truth I could do with a bit less of it myself. I've been tidying up quite a bit lately, not that anyone would ever notice; my room still looks like a bomb's just gone off.

The blue-and-white 'McMichael & Son, all your transportation requirements' bus lurched around the corner. That slogan is so dumb. We're talking about a third-rate busline that delivers kids to school and takes them on excursions. What sane person would choose to travel with masses of kids, complete with stale crusts and smelly feet? If I were given a choice, any other form of transport ever invented would win. 'McMichael & Son, for complete morons' would be nearer the mark.

The bus groaned to a halt. When the doors hissed open we saw why. Bodies were crammed to the roof, and there wasn't enough space for a budgie, let alone three hefty eleven year olds. Actually Rose had turned twelve, but you get the point. The driver had his greasy blue cap on backwards, the poser. He glared at us with blood-shot eyes, his skinny lips looking very mean.

'You lot'll haf to wade for the 806,' he drawled. His eyes didn't seem to open properly.

'But this is our bus! We'll be late if we go on the 806,' shouted Rose, who always stands up for herself. Sharon and I, like two wimps, were generally apologising for being alive.

'What a pity,' sneered the driver.

I was feeling very strange, and wondered if I might have a serious disease. I was burning up. Something wriggled up from the ground and exploded inside my skull. I found myself eye-balling the driver.

'What's your problem, Shorty?' he snarled. 'Are you deaf, stupid or both?'

I don't know what made me go up those steps, and as far as I was concerned it was the right time to scuttle down them again. Unfortunately that is not exactly what happened.

'Are you listening hard, because I'm only going to say this once? It's not MY problem, it's yours! This is our bus, Ferret Features, and if this crummy company loses our custom you won't be finding anyone else

stupid enough to travel like this. Have you thought of that?'

I was just about to stammer an apology but I had no idea whether I'd resumed control of my mouth.

Then a weird event unfolded before our eyes, though quite where else it might unfold is difficult to say. The driver shook his head from side to side as if he were trying to work out where he was, after waking from a heavy sleep. There was no colour in his face at all, which made his bloodshot eyes look even more unattractive. A small dribble trail wobbled down his chin. With absolutely no warning he lurched up from his seat and pushed a dozen kids off the bus.

'Wade for the 806,' he muttered, kicking a pile of bags after them.

He escorted me on board and Rose and Sharon wasted no time scuttling in behind. We drove away, leaving the kids on the pavement standing with their mouths gaping like a bunch of goldfish.

When we reached our usual stop, the bus kept right on going up the main driveway.

After we got out he drove away in a cloud of exhaust, scattering kids left and right. Mainly right, though, presumably because of the brick wall!

Our Principal, Miss Knight, is all right; she's strict but fair. Mr Endicott, the Deputy Principal, is a total creep, and is always on the lookout to see what you've done wrong. He enjoys searching lockers and stray schoolbags. Rubbish bins are his special favourite, and if he finds you've thrown your lunch away he makes you get it out and eat it. He must spend hours a day just looking out of his office window waiting to pounce. So of course he appeared, right on cue. Mr Endicott B.Ed. (Admin.), Dr of Peering (Hon). He was red with fury, eyeballs rolling, trusty notebook in hand. He certainly didn't waste time saying 'Good morning'.

'Why did that bus come in here? "No vehicles any time — ABSOLUTELY no exceptions". That's what the sign says' (and Mr Endicott should know, he painted it himself). 'Can't the man read? What does he think he's playing at?'

He spluttered on and on. Hard to ignore,

impossible to avoid being drenched by a fine spray of spit.

'Oh look, it's raining, sir,' said Rose with innocent eyes, an expression she's perfected. The eyeballs swivelled in her direction but the interrogation continued.

'Did any of you notice the registration plates? Was the driver wearing a name tag? Did anyone recognise him?' You'd think we'd been involved in a bank robbery at the very least!

'No, sir, he's not our usual driver, and he was acting real strange, sir,' volunteered Rose.

'Really strange,' corrected Mr Endicott mechanically.

'Yes, sir, he was,' agreed Rose, surprised but enthusiastic.

'No, no, you stupid girl, *really* strange not *real* strange.'

Rose is shameless. 'Yes, sir, I see. Well he was really pale, sir, and his eyes were really red and squinty, and we were really surprised when he drove up here, we told him not to.'

'Hmm, I see. Disgraceful. Danger to life and limb. The driver must be called to account for his actions. Let me assure you he will be feeling *real* sick by the time I'm finished with him. Heh … ehh … erkk … golp.'

That rusty, creaking groan was Mr Endicott laughing at his own pathetic joke. You've always got to be on guard though. His beady eyes rolled round.

'Good to see you wearing the correct ribbon, Nicola; good to see you wearing a ribbon at all. Heh, heh.' (Two jokes in one day, it must be the end of the world!)

'What has happened to that pocket?' This was not the sort of question you have to answer, so I waited.

'Yes, well get it mended. Very well, girls, don't let me hold you up. We don't want to be late for class.'

Then he rushed back up the steps for another strenuous bout of peering.

'Well, girls,' said Sharon dreamily, 'it beats me how anyone with so little hair could produce so much dandruff.' This observation was typical of Sharon's analytical approach to life.

I turned to Rose. 'You phony, how could you crawl like that? It was disgusting.' Rose flicked her hair back in what she thinks is a cool way — one day someone will tell her she's wrong.

'I had to say something; the two of you were acting like zombies.'

'Well wasn't it so lucky you were here then. Rosy Posy was really helpful, wasn't she, Sharon? Can we call you Rosy Posy, sweetheart?'

I ducked just in time to avoid most of her swinging arm.

'Is that a "No"?'

As usual, Sharon totally ignored our childish behaviour. 'How did you do that trick with the driver, Nick? "Ferret Features". Did you make that up? What about those kids he chucked off the bus? I'll never forget their faces.'

I stopped outside the toilet with my head spinning and yet another ruined hairstyle. What's new?

'Ferret Features? Never heard it before, not even from Dad.'

'But you said it.'

'Did I? I have to go in here, thanks to Rosy Posy's personality disorder. See you two in class.'

The toilet smelt like it usually does; an exciting mixture of urine, yellow cakes of disinfectant, soggy toilet paper, and wet concrete. The aroma is unmistakable. Anyone who tells you schooldays are the best days of your life has obviously forgotten it.

Round eyes watched from the spattered mirror. The eyes looked worried, probably because they were. I made sure my lucky chain was tucked inside my collar because we're not allowed to wear jewellery, and began brushing my hair for the second time in an hour, which probably created some sort of record.

'Excuse me, sir. Could we possibly squeeze in somewhere?' That was what I'd meant to say. Pretty stupid really, because anyone could see that we couldn't. Then I opened my mouth to find someone else directing the traffic. Those worried brown eyes were beginning to irritate me big time, reminding me of a day I'd tried very hard to forget. And now I couldn't …

About a month ago, Mum dragged me out of my nice warm bed to buy a pair of school shoes that I didn't need. My old ones were a bit worn, it's true, but there were no holes and the soles weren't flapping or anything. We don't see eye to eye on footwear. A very long morning was threatened as Mum stuffed the parking meter with coins.

'Three hours?'

'I know you!' she replied darkly.

A human fruit-bowl approached, which turned out to be dear Mrs Jacobs, my preschool teacher. I adored her. For my whole year of pre-school I wore hats: from the op shop, the dress-up box or anywhere else I could get my hands on them. Mrs Jacobs had a fantastic collection; she wore a different one every day. Every kid in the class loved her hats.

'Hello, Nicky. How lovely to see you, and aren't you getting tall?' She never forgets any-one.

I opened my mouth to say, 'Hello, Mrs Jacobs. How are you?' but that's not what came out.

'Good morning, Mrs Jay. Now listen up, I'm only saying this once. Do you realise that hat turns you into a figure of ridicule? It makes you look your age — and then some — possibly Elle Macpherson could get away with it, but come to think of it she's getting on a bit herself so she probably couldn't wear it either.'

It couldn't have been me, I don't even use

words like 'ridicule', but unfortunately, when words come out of your mouth people make this assumption you've said them.

Mrs Jacobs turned scarlet, Mum turned purple, and I turned white. I think Mrs Jay's eyes filled with tears, too; she walked away very fast.

Mum was fuming. She got the idea (and here she's a bit like those guinea fowl, once she gets an idea in her head there's not a great chance of shifting it) that I'd been deliberately rude to Mrs Jacobs because I didn't like Mum telling me which shoes I could have. It really didn't make a lot of sense. I had no idea what had happened myself, so there wasn't much chance of explaining anyway. After one look at her face I didn't even try.

You can imagine the happy time we had that morning. Dragged from shop to shop, I felt like one of those dogs that have to wear a muzzle in public because they've taken a chunk out of some little brat. Though I didn't pee on any lamp-posts or give anyone the teeniest nip, the way Mum acted you'd have thought I was the most vicious pit-bull terrier that ever lived.

We didn't even get any morning tea — that's how mad she was — and you should have seen the shoes! They were so gross I couldn't believe she was serious.

Even worse than the shoes was ringing up Mrs Jacobs to apologise. She was so nice about it! I wished that she'd yell or something, but a lovely woman like that probably doesn't know how to. It made me feel like the lowest sort of wormy reptile ever invented, which is why I'd tried to forget about it as quickly as possible.

This morning hadn't been *that* bad, but it was worrying that it had happened again. No time to think about it now, though. I get very bored with hurrying sometimes.

'Ah, Class 6B, welcome Nicky with a round of applause. Just a teeny bit late today. I trust you've had no difficult encounters with the wilder side of life this morning?'

I get really sick of Mrs Hammond sometimes, and I'd love to wipe that smirk off Marina Blair's face, she's such a creep, but she'll keep.

Sharon and Rose have big mouths! Recess was a nightmare.

'Here she is!'

'Nicky, come over here.'

'What happened?'

'Hey, did you hypnotise the driver?'

Everyone clustered around yelling questions at me.

'What's your secret? Come on, you can tell me?' (And me, and me …)

'Come on, aren't I your best buddy?' (Not the last time I looked.)

My fame had spread far and wide, but being a celebrity definitely has its downside. I didn't even get a chance to eat my little lunch, and I had the worst headache.

The next day we heard about the bus driver. McMichaels had been swamped with parents ringing to complain about their little darlings being dumped by the roadside, not to mention the ones who ended up with the wrong bag. Unfortunately a lot of money and expensive equipment went astray — into the pockets of some of the dear little victims, no doubt. One school went so far as to arrange trauma counselling at the bus company's expense, and Mr Endicott insisted that the driver had put our innocent little lives in peril by driving up to the office. How two-faced is that? You never hear the word 'innocent' mentioned when he looks in your locker.

The old 'danger to life and limb' routine must have worked though, because McMichaels sacked Greasy Cap. We heard that he'd been driving for over ten years without a complaint and never even had a day off sick in all that time, so that's loyalty for you. I wasn't griefstricken exactly; he hadn't treated us very well, but everyone's entitled to a bad day once in a while.

And you can't go around saying whatever comes into your head, can you? Not unless you're three years old.

2

There's not much you can do about parents.
They're so dumb about anything important.
They think they're keeping in touch with regular
interrogation sessions, but they get it all wrong:

'What's her name? She looks nice.' (The
class nerd.)

'What did you do at school today?' (Have
they really forgotten?)

'Did you eat your lunch?' (Give me a break,
what else would I do with it?)

'Tell me what you learnt at school today.' Once we had to write about this. I scored C–, my worst mark ever:

School is about rules; 'Don't spit in the corridor', 'No fighting in hallways', 'Do not throw food'. These rules tempt you to do things that would never have occurred to you otherwise. You develop many important skills at school, including crawling to people (teachers) you don't like, sitting inside wasting beautiful days, and eating from a lunchbox that could provide important evidence in your next science lesson on moulds and bacteria. Learning doesn't figure that much, most of the knowledge that you pick up through your life probably comes from reading, talking to your friends, watching television, surfing the net or going to theme parks. My advice, for what it's worth, is don't listen to them — make up your own mind!

I'm proud of the last part, but I didn't bother to show this to my parents, given our different outlook.

Parents and kids rarely talk, because whenever you want to talk to them there's all this stuff about how busy they are.

'Can't you see I'm reading the paper?'

'Not now dear, I'm cooking.' (Doing two things at once is a problem, is it?)

'Sorry, darling, give me ten minutes, I have to make a phone call.' (Make that three.)

So you try to catch one or other between phone calls on takeaway night during a journalists' strike! I tried for days.

Dad's always tired after work. You have to tiptoe around so as not to disturb him. He gets really stroppy if you so much as change the TV channel. He watches such boring programs, often with his eyes shut. I don't know what his problem is.

Mum's even more infuriating. She has this habit of conversing in stereo, like this:

'Amazing, dear' (not paying attention, bright and breezy).

'I don't know what has happened to your cricket socks, Paul, I only have one and it's a rather disgusting shade of green' (grumpy, holding up offending sock).

'Nicky, darling, you must be exaggerating.'

'This is absolutely the last time I'm forking out $25 for a new pair. You'll just have to play barefoot' (snarling, clenched teeth). 'It's no good taking that tone with me.'

It doesn't make a lot of sense even when you're there. I was the only one really trying. Paul has this way of grunting. He reckons Mum calms down quicker if he doesn't say anything to annoy her. I tried it once, but my grunts can't have captured quite the right tone because I was taken to the doctor for a thorough checkup.

I know when I'm beaten. After all, not many people can successfully compete with one green cricket sock.

I grabbed a large bar of chocolate from the cupboard because I always pig out when I'm depressed. After eating it very quickly, I was depressed *and* ready to throw up. Which may explain why I made one of the strangest decisions of my life: to ask big brother's advice, possibly a contradiction in terms.

Paul was lying with his head on the floor and his smelly socks on the pillow. He was clearly so shocked to see me that he forgot to say 'Get lost!' which was a good start, I thought. He's two years older than me — or twenty-eight months to be exact — but immature like all males. I kind of think of us as the same age, even though he acts like we're from different generations.

'Why are you upside down?'

He was playing a new game called 'Witches & Warlocks' so he didn't answer for ages — he's totally addicted.

'Yep! Best score ever, look at that.' He shoved the Gameboy under my nose. Since I'm not abnormally shortsighted, I couldn't see a thing. I took his word for it anyway because I wanted him in a good mood.

'It's easier to see the tracks through the maze upside down,' he explained. I was about to say, 'so what', but then remembered I'd asked what he was doing.

'Here, have a go, you won't beat my score.'

He likes to keep me in what he imagines is my place, somewhere between grovelling and snivelling. I don't give him much satisfaction if I can help it.

I settled myself upside down, which turned out to be quite comfortable. It was amazing how much clearer it was!

'How weird! Hey, does everyone know about this?'

'Shouldn't think so, and don't go spreading it around. It doesn't always work anyway, "Hogstail" is much harder upside down. Hey, you've had enough practice, get on with the game.'

'Feeling a little insecure, are we? All right, I'm ready now, so don't talk.'

I concentrated really hard, even though I was unlikely to beat Paul's score because he is pretty good, not that I'd ever admit it to him. Earning a little respect would be to my advantage so I carefully guided my broomstick through mazes haunted by monstrous figures. There were raging rivers, swamps full of crocodiles, and mountain passes guarded by dragons. It was so corny I could hardly restrain myself from insulting the intellects of those who waste time playing these games, but I needed Paul's help so I bit my tongue.

'You're not bad for a *girl*,' he said grudgingly, using the same tone as if he'd said *moron*. 'Did you want anything in particular?'

My attention wandered, and the last broomstick was zapped by a fork of lightning. I sat up, untangling some hair from my silver chain. It was a struggle to find the right words. When I was finished, he burst out laughing.

'Mum and Dad won't listen to me, and you're not taking it seriously. Families are supposed to stick together, offering strength and support in times of trouble. This isn't a family. We're just a bunch of people with nothing in common who don't even particularly like each other!'

'Is that an attack?' Paul asked enthusiastically.

'No, this is ME talking. Not that there's much point in opening my mouth around here!'

'Come on, Sis. It's not that bad. You're blowing it completely out of proportion. Girls are so over the top when they get emotional. All that's happened is you going around telling a few home truths. Maybe you've swallowed a truth drug. There's this rare vine that grows in the Amazon jungle — near the last remaining tribe of head hunters — it acts on the central nervous system and ...'

He's nuts about the environment, so I interrupted before he could get into full flow.

'I could say anything to anybody. It's not at all funny. In fact it's very embarrassing.'

Paul laughed even harder, the pig.

'What about when you told Mr Williams his dog was a mangy old flea factory? That was funny. Dad thought so too, even though he told you not to be so outspoken. I've got it! You've contracted the famous Outspoken's Disease.'

I was absolutely horrified, having completely forgotten about Mr Williams, a war veteran who lives down our street. He gets no visitors apart from Meals on Wheels. The only company he has is a disgusting little dog who passes the time by lifting his leg all over the place, farting explosively and biting the postman. This moth-eaten mongrel is probably the only reason Mr Williams is still alive.

'That's three times, and what about the other times I've forgotten?'

Paul was still chuckling to himself, the idiot. I don't know why I thought I'd get a sensible response from him anyway, I never have before.

'The bus driver's lost his job, Mrs Jacobs was deeply hurt, and Mr Williams probably hates me, how funny is that?' I was getting very angry. He stopped laughing and ruffled my hair, quite kindly for one who enjoys tormenting his little sister.

'Oh, it'll probably wear off, you know.'

Paul's not into wasting sympathy, though. He was playing a higher level of 'Witches & Warlocks' before I'd even left the room. I felt more alone than ever.

3

My next victim was David Walters. You might wonder why I'd pick on a harmless, prematurely bald, hardworking guy, which makes two of us. David is my Dad, the last person on earth I'd deliberately hurt.

Poor old Dad's a workaholic. He worries a lot about things like orthodontists and school fees. Being junior partner in a firm of accountants, Dad scores all the jobs no one else wants: 'Good old David will see to it!' From fixing up complicated balance sheets to interviewing painful clients that no one else wants to see, he's very willing.

And that's exactly what happens at home; another 'yuk' job, call for Dad! A recent case — and this is true — was Mum's decision to fertilise our garden with human sewage. She's always getting enthusiastic about something, and caught the greenie bug from Paul raving on. But all she had to do was use the compost bin and he'd have been ecstatic. Sometimes I think she's not all there.

'We'll get great results, darling. Think of the roses.'

'I've always been quite happy with dynamic lifter, Wendy.'

'But we're doing the harbour a big favour, David,' cooed Mum.

'Bugger the harbour,' he muttered.

I was shocked! Still it was good to see some fight in him.

'Darling?'

'Nothing, dear.' He gave her a tired smile. His shoulders drooped as he inspected two containers that had been deposited on our doorstep by a bunch of ferals early this morning. Vigilantes for a Cleaner World is what they call themselves, down at Wild & Free, Paul's second home.

'For all we know this is probably illegal.'

'Oh no, David. This is the government's bright new scheme to improve our waterways.'

'The downside being we have to give up our gardens, I suppose.'

Mum didn't hear, and I don't think Dad intended her to. He plodded off to begin the stinky task. Hours later I found him in a cloud of flies, burning his favourite gardening gear in our barbecue. I chose to look at it as one man's stand against the banning of backyard incinerators, but the truth is he probably couldn't think of any other way to get rid of the stink.

When I was younger I can remember him being a lot of fun. The main problem is his job, it sucks all the life out of him. But you never really know, he surprised everyone by signing up for a painting class recently. He used to do stuff like that, really ace black-and-white photographs, and there's some pottery and sculpture in the shed from years and years ago, before I was born. This painting thing came out of the blue though, and I was a bit worried about what it might lead to. You know, painting today, followed by spirituality and soybean fritters next week. Anyway, I decided to stop obsessing about it; if anyone deserves some fun it's Dad.

One foul winter afternoon, about a week after my little chat with Paul, I walked soggily home, having missed the bus again. Our place was crowded, all eyes glued to Dad's latest painting. Mum has this preschool idea that creativity must be encouraged at all costs! Our neighbour, George, made a few snorting noises, which could have meant anything, then he finished his coffee and left rather suddenly. Paul grinned wildly but said nothing. He was in rather a hurry to go somewhere too. That left me. What could I do but look?

The painting was about a metre square, and the subject was some sort of council meeting. For whatever reason, Dad had painted all the councillors in the nude, not a shred of clothing between them, except they all wore gumboots. You could tell which one was the the mayor by the gold chains that dangled down to his bulging belly. Dad could have been having a go at people who get off on telling everyone else what to do, but it was such a terrible painting that nothing else mattered. Murky globs of paint looked like they'd been slapped on with a trowel, and with such poor knowledge of the human body and no perspective at all it would be lucky to score a D in our art class.

'It's … interesting, don't you think, Nicky?' said Mum optimistically.

'It's symbolic,' Dad grinned, with all his teeth showing. His expression quickly changed to one of concern.

'Nicky, get out of those wet clothes immediately, you'll get pneumonia.'

I realised I was shivering; cold and then very hot, especially my face. Unfortunately it wasn't pneumonia though, it was *that* feeling again! Something fizzed up my backbone and crackled out of my fingertips, even my hair stood on end. I would have done anything to be somewhere else, or *someone else*.

I tried so hard to say something kind. If I shut my eyes and held my breath, nothing could happen. I opened my eyes again, confident the moment was over. Dad's little smirk didn't help. I sure wiped that off his face!

'If you like I'll tell you what I really think. That painting is the most revolting object I have ever seen. If you really painted it Dad, my only question is, WHY?'

As if that wasn't enough, I took a deep breath and continued the assault.

'Are you listening to me? This is obviously the work of someone emotionally disturbed, visually impaired, mentally unstable or possibly all three. Were your eyes shut, or did you hold the paintbrush with your armpit?'

Mum's horrified face came into focus. My stomach flipped hard against my backbone — part hunger pangs, part despair. I blundered out of the kitchen hunched over with misery. I heard Dad moan softly as I collapsed outside. Mum was comforting him.

'Don't worry, darling, we all like it. Nicky's not an expert' (Mum has this 'thing' about expert opinion). 'Let's face it, she knows nothing.'

'She's not the only one,' groaned Dad. 'How can I face the class? They must think I'm a complete cretin. I even boasted about this pile of shit.'

Mum tells us off for swearing — she's very strict like that — but she didn't say a word this time. Dad went on analysing the painting over and over, getting more depressed each time, and I wasn't feeling that flash myself. I went upstairs and burrowed under my doona, counting the minutes until Mum came thundering in, breathing fire. I even knew what she'd say!

'I've come to give you a piece of my mind, young lady.'

'You needn't bother, I've given it to myself already, and I still wish I was dead.'

Mum looked even angrier than ever. I'd hit the jackpot this time. She has this little fold on the outside of her lips that is usually invisible, but right now it rivalled the Grand Canyon. I was so upset I didn't even care.

'This is why I've been trying to talk to you. You never listen. I didn't *mean* any of that stuff. I wanted to say "How original", "You're so creative, Dad," but it came out wrong. That wasn't even me, I don't use words like that.'

Mum was quiet for a minute; perhaps she

felt sorry for me. As I stood up I caught sight of myself in the mirror, half-undressed, my eyes swollen and bloodshot from crying. Add a huge red nose and convulsive hiccups to the bird's-nest hairdo and you have a thoroughly miserable specimen. Mum's always so tidy: every hair in place, clothes colour co-ordinated and smoothly ironed. You could say we're opposites.

She swallowed hard, and made an obvious effort to talk more quietly, still yelling of course, but not as loud. 'It's difficult to imagine that you could be so unkind on purpose, but how can you seriously expect me to believe that fairy-tale?' (So she had been listening the other day — slightly.) 'I'm not a complete half-wit, Nicola.' This is one of Mum's phrases that you get used to; I wonder about it sometimes — can you have a complete half? Anyway, the important thing to remember when you hear this phrase is to say nothing. Which, of course, I didn't remember.

'But Mum, it's all true what I told you. You have to believe me. At least Paul listened, he thinks it's a big joke. It isn't funny, I feel like an unexploded bomb, and I never know when I'm going to blow up next.'

Mum stared at me, obviously deciding I'd totally flipped. 'You've been *talking* to Paul?'

I knew she was trying, but it was like she couldn't comprehend what I was saying. Establishing that I'd been forced to talk to Paul at least made her realise I was desperate.

Finally she said, 'Yes, well, you'll have to stay in your bedroom for now. This state of affairs cannot be allowed to continue. I will talk to your father immediately.'

'OK, Mum. Tell him I'm really sorry, please. I feel so bad. You have to say that.'

She frowned importantly, not wanting to give the impression I was being let off the hook. She's very transparent. Then she nodded and walked out, carrying a couple of the bricks I'd been carting around for the last few weeks. The things you have to do in this house to get any-one to listen!

4

At teatime I was released on a good behaviour bond. Paul told a few antique jokes but it was not the most fun evening in living memory.

'What's the definition of an Irish torch, Mum?'

'How would I know? I'm not Irish,' she snapped back.

'But you're blonde though,' replied Paul, which sailed right over Mum's head.

'Dad?'

'Herumph, what?'

'Give up? Any last-minute thoughts? Nicky? Well, I'll have to tell you then. Da da! A solar-powered one.'

As Paul's attempt at wit did nothing to lighten up the atmosphere, he gave up, and began talking to himself instead. Dad was staring at his plate in a stunned sort of way. Mum kept asking him if he was all right, did he have enough to eat, how did he rate the flavour and texture on a satisfaction scale from 1 to 10.

Finally Dad reached saturation point — it had to happen — he slammed both fists onto the table and yelled at the top of his voice, 'The food is fine, the wine is perfect, the cutlery's gleaming, the pepper is impeccable and the salt irresistible. Everything's bloody marvellous!'

Then he stormed out of the room. We heard our front door slam and the screech of rubber. In the silence that followed Mum looked from me to Paul and back.

'Now see what you've done,' she accused no one in particular.

'Surely my jokes weren't that bad?' Paul winked at me.

'It wasn't the jokes, it was the company, me in particular.' I began to clear away the plates.

'Ohhh! So that's why you're imitating a two-dimensional form. I thought it must be the latest science topic; test the following: At which point is a humanoid able to slip through a crack in the average floorboard? Plot your answer on a cartesian plane.'

'Oh shut up, Paul,' said Mum uncharacteristically. She took the words right out of my mouth. Paul slouched over to the TV.

'Well I just live here, don't bother to tell me anything.' He flipped through the channels several times, perhaps hoping the programs on offer would become more to his liking than they were thirty seconds ago. Obviously not, though, because he switched off.

'I think I'll go and have lots of fun counting the mould spores on my football boots. Yes, Mum, before you ask, I found them in Barry's sports bag and I have absolutely no idea how they got there. Failing that, I'll just murder a few zits … splattt.'

'Getting out of the dishes: Method 785,' I thought sourly, as he clattered upstairs.

There's something a bit offputting about smoke escaping from the ears of the person next to you; it's not very relaxing. I didn't particularly like muttered insults or the glares either, so I cleared up in record time.

I couldn't think of anything to do after that, apart from going to bed. Pathetic really, it was only eight o'clock, but I was tired. The next thing I knew the sun was shining into my eyes, which caused a minor panic attack until I remembered it was Saturday. I wanted breakfast badly, but how to get it without being spotted?

This proved to be Mission Impossible because my parents were in occupation of the kitchen, and the bench was littered with dirty mugs. Either they'd been up for hours or several dozen people had come to breakfast. I sidled in close to the wall, doing my best to act invisible. Dad smiled, but Mum was still several degrees below permafrost. Her voice was unfriendly and her eyes were cold.

'Nicky, your father and I have had a long discussion.' Dad grinned and gestured to the mess on the bench. 'In the course of which we both recollected several attempts you made to communicate. For a variety of reasons we were unable to respond.'

'Cut it out, Wendy, you sound like a lawyer,' said Dad in his normal, nice voice.

'Come and sit here, Nicky. Don't look at me with those scared bunny eyes. You did me a favour. The more I think about it the more I realise that I have to thank you.'

'Thank me? I was horrible and despicable and repulsive. You have to believe that I didn't mean it.' My eyes filled with tears, what a wuss!

Dad took my hand in both of his. 'Yes, Nicky, thank you. The painting is all the things you said, and more. I needed someone to be straight with me.' His face clouded. 'Unhappily most people are not completely truthful. It's a way of the world to tell little white lies to protect people's feelings or sometimes to avoid embarrassment. Of course there are times one needs to display tact and diplomacy, but it would be refreshing if everyone was more straightforward. If you can't expect honesty in your own home what hope is there? That's why I want to thank you for telling me the truth.' He looked pained. 'My only regret is I didn't ask your opinion before parading that thing all over the office.' He shut his eyes and shuddered.

Dad seemed different, more open some- how. I remembered how he used to play with me when I was little; he's the one who made up the game Chocs & Robbers; we played that all the time. I gave him a huge hug. I wanted him to know how sorry I was; it was easier than trying to explain my jumbled mess of feelings. We sat there grinning like idiots at each other. It was like he understood what was happening to me — which was a bit more than I did, actually.

'Look, Nicky, of course David has a point, but you simply can't go around offending people willy nilly.' (Where does she get those expres- sions of hers?) 'Mrs Jacobs's hat was appalling, but it wasn't worthwhile telling her; presumably she likes hideous hats!'

'But, but …' I stammered, feeling tears pricking the back of my eyes and an enormous lump in my throat. Sometimes I hate my mother, she always manages to miss the most important point. It was really annoying that now I had their undivided attention I couldn't think of a thing to say.

I took a deep breath and tried anyway.

'But you're not seeing the worst part, I didn't mean it about the hat — I wasn't even thinking about it — I can't control my own mouth when it happens. It's like someone else speaking, they're not even words I use. Look at what I said about Dad's painting, it sounded more like Mr Endicott than me! It's not just about being honest, it's like being possessed, now do you see the problem?'

I'd succeeded in frightening everyone in the room, especially myself. Mum and Dad looked at each other across the trail of cups.

'All right, Nick, go outside and ride your bike or something. We'll talk some more and come up with a solution.'

Mum sounded casual but it had to be fake, judging by the loaded looks she was shooting at Dad.

I looked down at the clump of cornflakes in my bowl, about as appetising as the old chewie you find stuck under the benches at school. It wasn't like Mum to let me escape without finishing breakfast. In any case, she knows perfectly well the love affair with my bike ended that day I rode down the steps at our local park. On the second last step I fell over the handlebars and broke my wrist, chipped two front teeth, grazed just about everything and narrowly avoiding falling in the river. It's really not too surprising that I haven't been near my bike since. Apart from anything else, the front wheel is not what it used to be. Mum had the major freakout of all time when she found out I wasn't wearing my helmet. A totally irrelevant detail considering my head was the only undamaged part of my whole body.

Mum's absentmindedness convinced me that she was taking my problem seriously, at last. I went outside feeling more hopeful. They'd think of something, wouldn't they?

A few days later I found out what that 'something' was and I wasn't impressed! Running late as usual, I galloped downstairs to be met by one of Mum's understanding smiles, a terrifying experience on an empty stomach!

'I don't like it,' said Paul, apparently to the organic bricks in his bowl. Who could blame him? It looked revolting. He was crouched over reading the cereal box — again.

'What's up?' I hissed.

He raised his head just far enough for me to see his eyes rolling upwards until all that was visible were white, veiny eyeballs. I think that meant he didn't know anything.

'Hurry up, Paul, you'll be late,' snapped Mum, drifting in carrying a plate piled high with toast.

'It must be you who's the object of all this love and attention. What a relief!' Paul grabbed some toast on his way out, collecting a cuff to the side of his head as well.

'Now then, darling, you must have a good breakfast. Here, have some,' she said. I told you about her split personality!

'Haffn't any time.' But I gulped down some orange juice and grabbed a piece of the toast to calm her down. 'Yuk! I hate toast and Vegemite.'

'Don't be ridiculous, Nicky, everyone likes toast with Vegemite. Slow down and take your time. Here, give me that plate.'

Mum's sometimes just like one of those garbage-disposal thingies in the sink, though maybe not as noisy. Paul came back to get his lunch just as Mum presented me with another plateful.

'I can't possibly eat this, I'm not even hungry,' I wailed. 'I have to go now.'

'You need a good breakfast to get your metabolism going,' Mum cooed, simultaneously slapping Paul hard as he reached over for the top two slices.

'They're not for you, and you've just brushed your teeth.' Paul glared at her and rubbed the back of his hand.

'You're feral, Mum.'

'What's so special about my metabolism anyway? And if I've got to eat this I'll need some chocolate spread.' Mum groaned; she thinks chocolate spread is *so* unhealthy, but she passed me the jar with another of those sinister smiles.

'You're not going to school this morning, Nicky. We're going to meet … meet a really … a really NICE … man.'

She'd obviously flipped.

'Have you forgotten a minor detail? I'm eleven, not four. I go to school now. I can't meet whoever his name is today anyway; we're doing a play. To get a good part I absolutely have to be there.'

'I'll come to meet the nice man, Mummy.' Paul's ears were flapping vigorously; he was obviously getting ready for takeoff!

'Nick off, Dumbo,' I said. Mummy looked ever so slightly fed up.

'That's quite enough from both of you. Paul, for goodness sake go to school. Nicky, you're coming with me to see a special doctor, if you must know. Nothing dramatic, he just wants to chat. I'm going to get ready. Just humour me, and eat some of that toast.'

'The nice man won't mind seeing you in your dressing gown, Mummy.' Paul was being such a pain I felt like strangling him. Pity there's a law against it.

'I don't need to see any doctor. I'm not sick,' I shouted at the back of Mum's head.

Marina Blair would get the best part in the play and I'd score something exciting like third passerby and have to put up with her gloating.

Paul leaned over.

'You're going to see a very special doctor, sweetheart,' he lisped, imitating Mum. 'A doctor for ever-so-slightly nutty people. Isn't that lovely?'

Then he added, 'She's taking you to a shrink,' in his normal obnoxious voice, patting my cheek so hard it made my eyes water.

I thought of throwing a glass of orange juice at him but settled on a piece of toast. Unbelievably, this hit the target and a thick lump of chocolate glued itself to his hat. The thought of Paul walking into school with a discarded crust on his head was far and away the best thing that had happened today, not that there was much competition.

'Good riddance,' I thought, as he slammed out of the door whistling. 'I'm not nutty. What are they playing at? This is what happens when you treat parents as equals. I should have kept my mouth shut.' Then I realised what I'd said. If only it was that easy!

5

'Nicky, darling, say hello to Dr Roobottom.'

My mouth must have been hanging open, because Mum nudged me hard in the ribs. No wonder he was a shrink, he must have had to practise on himself after dragging a name like that around. At first Mum did all the talking, but that was soon fixed.

'Now, Wendy, may I call you that?' (Not a lot she could do about it really.) 'Wendy, Wendy, what am I going to do with you? Why not go and put your feet up in the waiting room? My receptionist will make you a healthy and refreshing cup of herbal tea. Nicky and I will get on so much better without you.'

Mum didn't like being treated as a problem. It was funny to see her in the role of stubborn kid for a change.

'Well, if you're quite sure? Yes. I suppose you know what you're doing and if you need me I'll be right outside.'

Roobottom made it clear that this was most unlikely, and Mum wandered out. The Doc didn't say anything for ages; he was smiling at a pile of papers on his desk.

To fill in the time I had a daydream about that name. The founder of the clan, Sir Rupert Rowebotthamley, was probably a mate of King Arthur and his merry men. After a few centuries of plundering innocent bystanders, the family became known as the Rowbothams of Ramsgate, and they were seriously rich and famous. A couple of hundred years ago, one of their black sheep disgraced himself and ended up halfway across the world with a bunch of convicts and a whole lot of other sheep. The name has changed a bit over the years, as is usually the case; future generations may end up as the Roobums of Rathdowney. Then again, I could be looking at the end of the line!

I looked around at his leather-topped desk, the rows of books bound in blue, the full-length velvet curtains, and the creamy yak-fur broadloom. Even the pen-and-pencil desk-set was goldplated, with a few gems carelessly attached, just like one of those useless prizes on 'Sale of the Century'. This guy was seriously loaded.

'You're very bossy,' I said abruptly.

He blinked and looked a bit surprised, maybe he didn't know!

'Mothers can be such a drag, they talk and talk. You know the story,' he said.

Well I know yours, Roobum. You're trying to get me on side by bagging Mum! I didn't say anything, so he probably thought he had me eating out of his hand.

'You are free to talk with me about anything at all, Nicky. Hobbies, your friends and enemies, parents, school, anything you like. My side of the bargain is to listen and not interrupt. How does that sound?'

'Pretty straightforward' from your point of view! If either of my parents had said half as much a week ago I'd have been over the moon, now I was a seriously long way from ecstatic.

'You mean I can say anything about anything?' He nodded so energetically that I thought his glasses would fall off; they were gold-framed and made him look like a dentist.

Deciding to play along, I described long-ago holidays, TV programs, the major crazes of Grade 3 — bubblegum cards and gross Shetland ponies with rainbow manes — food I hate, films I like, books I've read, you name it. Never once in all this garbage did I mention the reason I was here. I expected him to interrupt with 'OK, Nicky, let's cut the crap and get on with the real stuff!' But he never said a word.

I droned on and on in that expensive room.

When I finally looked at Dr Roobottom, his eyes were closed and he was rocking gently backwards and forwards, obviously thinking up his Lotto numbers. I stopped mid-drivel to see what would happen.

Nothing is what happened, total silence!

'You certainly are a great listener,' I said loudly. He jumped a little and rubbed his gold specs, probably to give himself time to wake up.

'Hmm? Hmmm? That's my job description in a manner of speaking.'

Nice work if you can get it. Nodding off in a comfortable chair, earning $200 an hour while you do it.

An alarm pealed somewhere, and Dr Roobottom came to life in a seriously weird way. Leaping up, he grabbed my arm and hustled me into the waiting room. The meter for those well-developed listening skills had obviously expired!

The receptionist had made Mum a pot of revolting mint and lime herbal tea which she was too polite not to drink. She looked anxious and slightly green.

'Hello, Doctor,' she said eagerly, 'have you found out anything yet?'

He made a brushing motion with his hand as if shooing off an irritating fly.

'We've made excellent progress for the first session, Mrs Walters.' (What happened to Wendy, Wendy?) 'I'll see Nicola again next week. Linda looked after you I hope? Good, good.'

He clasped Mum's shoulders and gazed deeply into her eyes. 'We mustn't — indeed cannot — hurry nature, my dear Mrs Walters.'

He smeared us both with a greasy smile, and disappeared.

His next patient, a vague-looking stick man, was counting his collection of used bus and train tickets and writing the tally in a small notebook before beginning all over again. He was very intent and did not look up. Friendly Linda rolled her eyes in his direction, and tapped the side of her head meaningfully.

'Brian's been coming here for two years,' she hissed. 'Mad as a hatter.'

I began to feel sorry for Brian Bus Tickets. I felt in urgent need of some counselling myself, after an hour and a half. What state would I be in after two years?

6

'Did you have a good session with Dr Roobottom, Nicky?'

On the way home Mum's tongue was hanging out with curiosity. Nothing had happened one way or the other. A total waste of time is how I'd honestly describe it. Not being in one of my 'truthful' moods I decided to say nothing.

My next appointment was after school, which was a small improvement. At least I didn't have to explain to the other kids where I was going.

After three weeks of strenuous verbal exercise for me and restful snoozes for the Doc, I decided he'd been ripping Mum and Dad off for long enough.

The fourth week he greeted me as usual, and settled back comfortably in his impossibly expensive, genuine Italian leather armchair with his eyes closed.

'Dr Roobottom,' I said loudly, hoping to eject him from his comfort zone. 'I'm going to level with you.' He looked shocked. This wasn't in the script.

'It's about this awkward habit,' — dramatic pause — might as well practise for my pathetic part in the play. 'No, awkward isn't right, excruciatingly embarrassing is more like it. See, I sometimes tell people exactly what I'm thinking. You know how ideas flash around, like sort of brainwaves. You don't even pay much attention to them yourself, right? Well, what happens is sometimes I have no control. I say some of those ideas out loud, without meaning to, and sort of worse than I'd ever thought them. That can't be right, it's my mouth and I should know what it's about to say. Anyhow, it doesn't last very long and isn't regular or anything. I always hope it's gone away, then WHAM!'

Dr Roobottom was looking a bit startled; well, at least his eyes were open. Perhaps because I was in the habit of yakking to him I rattled on with everything, finishing with that brilliant demolition job on Dad's self-confidence. Though the Doc's mouth twitched when I described the painting, his face immediately returned to its usual blank. He was rocking to and fro all the time, which for some reason reminded me of a baby sucking a dummy. I was feeling totally off after reminding myself of this most recent gush of truthfulness.

I stopped talking, and waited for a response. Anything. He just sat there and looked at me, rocking and rocking.

'The good listening thing can be carried too far you know,' I shouted. 'What I need now is answers. Like, am I crazy or not?'

He looked down, and inspected his fingernails for a while.

'What an interesting story,' he said finally.

'I don't think I've ever heard of a case like this before.'

He was leaning forward on his elbows, making this funny humming noise. Then he pressed his knuckles together very carefully, as if he'd never done it before and was amazed. I suppose if you listen to nutty people day after day it must rub off, even supposing you were all there in the first place, and by now I had my doubts.

I wriggled about in my chair, nothing at all like the one his side of the desk. All that waiting was getting to me.

'What's the cure then?' I demanded.

'Hmm, let me see now. How shall I explain this in simple terms?'

It looked like he was talking to the desk calendar. Then he actually looked at me. I hadn't noticed before, but his eyes — which were small and close together — were the clearest, midsummer blue. A total waste really, since he hardly ever looked at anyone; they might just as well have been white.

'What is happening from *temps à temps*' (what a poser) 'is that your preconditioned socialisation techniques are overidden; just as an electrical safety switch disables a series of power points if a leakage of electric current occurs.'

'But, since I'd be a lot safer if it didn't happen, it's really an *un*safety switch. Who's ever heard of that?' I screeched.

He continued as if I hadn't spoken.

'You then respond aggressively, essentially in antisocial mode,' he continued, smiling moronically. 'In other words, you say what you mean rather than that which is socially acceptable. While at university, I was highly attracted to the School of Naturopathy, attending many lectures when I had free time' (now I *knew* he was a fruit loop). 'The point you make of feeling overheated during an attack is indicative. With my very basic understanding of such matters I would hazard a guess that your thyroid gland may be underactive, which in turn may cause spasms of overactivity in the attempt to find balance that all living creatures crave.' He didn't actually say 'Praise the Lord', but you get what I mean. 'Tell your mother that kelp tablets may be very beneficial, she will find them at any good health food store.'

'Oh don't worry about that, our local health food shop is her second home.'

The alarm pealed.

'That's all we have time for today, but we're making excellent progress,' he said, grabbing me by the elbow.

'But is there a cure? I must have an answer before next week.' I was begging.

'Let's not mention the word *cure*. After all, that gives the impression of ill health. We'll approach these undesirable behaviours as a challenge, discovering together some ways to modify or bypass this highly individual personality permutation of yours. We must not rush though. These things take time. Have patience.'

'A patient patient, that's me,' I said gloomily.

He chuckled at this sorry attempt at humour as I was forcibly expelled into the waiting room.

'I think we may be getting somewhere,' I told Mum on the way home. She probably needed a boost, I knew I did!

'What did he say, Nicky?'

'Oh, he gabbled on about electricity and

switches and balance,' I hedged. 'Then he said to be patient, and that kelp tablets might help.'

'But you were in there an hour and a half,' she pleaded desperately. 'He must have said more than that.'

'He's a good listener.'

Mum sighed, probably because she was taking a long last look at our summer holiday before it disappeared into one of Dr Roobottom's designer pockets.

7

Visiting Dr Roobottom was now part of my week. Not the best part, but probably not the worst either, as there's always something disgusting happening at school.

Sports Day was coming up, and I wasn't much looking forward to that. All the yelling and screaming gives me a headache, and I usually manage to sit on an ants' nest. When I was young I made up a sort of motto: 'Please God, make me not come last!' Paul still stirs me about it. He reckons I recited it for three weeks when I was in Grade 1. We used to share a room so it could be that he's telling the truth for once, but he doesn't have to go on and on. Just because he's a sock-sniffing, sports-crazy moron, and I'm not. I'm not *that* bad. I can swim and catch a ball and stuff, but I don't shine. What's more, I don't even care.

So what happened the day of the under-13 T-ball trials? My imbecilic side must have been dominating, because I let Rose talk me into trying out for the team. Spending time with Doc had obviously unbalanced me more than I realised.

Sharon and I walked down to the oval with Rose, doing her usual motivation bit. She obviously believes that one day I'll transform into a sport freak like her.

'Nicky, this will be fun!'

'D'ya reckon?'

'Everyone's different. This is probably the sport you've been waiting for.'

'Why?'

'Well, it combines running, throwing, catching and hitting. What could be better than that?' She was super-enthusiastic.

Sharon snorted. 'Something tells me that Nicky could provide several interesting answers to that question.'

We were both looking at Rose, whose face was a blank. She just didn't get it. The truth is that Sharon has more of a feel for reality than Rose. Although she's into sport herself, she has no trouble accepting that I'm not.

Then I saw something gross. Marina Blair was on the oval before us. I tried really hard not to vomit on my runners. You can have too much of some people. As if it wasn't enough for her to get the best part in our pathetic school play, she makes a habit of scoring last-second winning goals, can jump twice as high as anyone else, and knows what to do with a shot put just when you're hoping she'll drop it on her foot. She's so up herself it's a health hazard.

'Look who's here! I'm off.'

Sharon grabbed hold of my tracksuit.

'Don't you dare move,' said Rose. 'After all the trouble we've taken getting you here.' Rather unreasonable of her, I thought.

'You can't let that little creep get one over

you, Nick,' Sharon hissed in my ear. 'Don't give her the satisfaction.'

I looked over to where Marina stood surrounded by her usual gang, gawping gooses the lot of them. Marina was acting like she was deeply involved in what Sue-Ellen Marsh was saying. I knew that wasn't possible. Sue-Ellen's so boring she makes having a tetanus shot seem like fun. Every now and then Marina glanced over to check out what we were doing. I did what came naturally and totally ignored her.

The sports teacher, Ms Woodall, was busy applying several litres of sunscreen. It's true she does have that fair freckly skin that goes with red hair, but she really should consider buying a few shares in Le Tan the way she gets through that stuff. Sunsafe is great, I'm sure, but this was winter, thick grey clouds — what did she think was going to happen in twenty minutes?

'Help yourself, girls,' said Ms Woodall generously, beginning to mark our names off. Olive-skinned Marina, who's never been sunburnt in her whole life, slithered up and poured several buckets of lotion on herself. That girl will crawl anywhere in order to be noticed.

Ms Woodall then picked oily Marina to captain team A, and Rochelle Smart to captain team B. It hurts me to admit this, but Rochelle is quite possibly even more annoying than Marina. A pale copy, minus charisma.

Sharon groaned loudly as the two captains began picking their teams. At least they'd both want her!

I hate it, trying to act invisible and relaxed at the same time. As if you've had at least three better offers in the last half hour that you've decided to turn down. It never works. Somehow shameless pleading ('Pick me, can't you please pick me, don't leave me standing here on my own') is completely obvious to everyone within a 300 km radius.

First Rose and then Sharon were chosen. I stood on my own, deliberately looking off in the opposite direction, pretending I had more important things on my mind. Now I wonder what could be happening up by the library? Perhaps I should take a closer look. Shuffling cautiously backwards, I decided no one would notice if I disappeared.

Ms Woodall looked around and frowned.

'Stop scuffing up the grass, Nicola. Do you want a dustbowl for an oval?'

I'd gone off her in a big way! Asking questions without answers just like Mum does, and such a terrible judge of character. I mean, Marina and Rochelle, give me a break!

Then Marina looked over at me and smiled. I nearly keeled over on the spot.

'I choose Nicky. Come on, you can be our pitcher.'

I couldn't believe it. Marina was being nice to me.

I suppose it serves me right for not trusting my primal instincts about Rottweilers, funnel-web spiders and girls like Marina. Can you believe I actually smiled back? Walking over to her team, blushing with surprised relief? I'd been chosen. I wasn't going to be left on my own this time, equipment carrier, spare part, not fit to be in a team.

Then I heard the giggling. Even Ms Woodall was fighting a smile. Only Sharon and Rose didn't find anything to laugh at. Well, I told you that I don't find sport that fascinating. How was I to know there is no pitcher in T-ball?

What happens is that the batter hits the ball from a flat kind of stand thing, covered in rubber, and then takes off for first base. I found that out later, though; all I knew then was that Marina had won again.

I put my head down and walked over to the end of the bunch, imagining I was somewhere else. Even though I have a good imagination, this did not work.

'Your turn will come, Blair; your turn will surely come,' I thought, plastering a false smile on my face as Marina put her arm around me.

'Just a little joke, Nick. We're really happy to have you on our team, aren't we, girls?'

So many gleaming, fake smiles, nodding heads, happy to jump any way that Marina demanded, but she didn't fool me this time. Once maybe, but never again …

8

The day after I was picked as reserve for the reserve in the under-13 T-ball team, my weekly visit to Doc Roobottom rolled around. In my head I'd named him Robot — that's what he reminded me of: he was about as much use.

Mum developed a severe allergic reaction to Linda's tea after the first few weeks — she would insist on drinking the whole pot. Now she's learning everything there is to know about the local cafe scene — she's always wanted to be an expert in something, and you can drink a lot of coffee in an hour and a half. I've told her she should write a book. I've even thought of a title for her: *Caffeine and Me: My Life as an Addict*. But so far she hasn't been up to the challenge.

The humiliation of being joke-pitcher was still fresh in my mind and I whinged a bit about the disgustingness of Marina Blair.

When I heard snoring, my shattered self-confidence fell below zero. I could even bore a robot. When he woke up, the poser acted like falling asleep was part of his grand plan, allowing the subconscious to take over or something. I can't work that out, my subconscious is the one that needs examining, not his.

Then he asked some questions in gobbledegook.

'Have you the slightest notion what may invoke the characteristic inversions of your normal behaviour mode, Nicola?'

'Huh?' This was partly shock. It had been three weeks since I'd heard his voice.

'All behaviour has its roots somewhere in our lives. Our task now is to unearth the trigger.

What could that be?' His tiny blue eyes shone with enthusiasm. As Grandma says, There's nothing like a good nap to freshen you up.

'Now that you're awake, isn't it time *you* came up with some answers?' I said.

'Could that be an attack?' He looked very interested. I said a few rude words under my breath. The man was a waste of space.

About a month after that something really big happened to our robot–patient relationship. For no particular reason that I could see, Robot suddenly snapped to attention in a seriously weird way. One minute he was gazing lovingly at his bookcase, and the next he sat straight up and his teeny-weeny blue eyes bored twin holes in my skull.

'Enjoyable as our chats have been Nicola, I have been unable to discern any conclusive evidence of defective synapse activity, schizo-phrenic traits or patterns of psychosis. In fact, you appear to be, ermm, completely normal.'

He looked slightly disappointed that he'd been unable to come up with any major person-ality malfunction.

I was relieved of course, but also very angry.

After all, I'd been wasting my Friday afternoons for weeks, and I knew for a fact — Paul had steamed open one of his accounts — that the fees this guy charged were astronomical. Even Christmas was probably cancelled this year, and forget pocket money. We'd been eating stacks of soy beans too. For what?

'I'm sorry,' I snarled. *'That simply is not good enough. If you paid a plumber to fix your drain, how would you react if he fiddled around a little, left a disgusting mess, gave you a hefty bill or two, and then said he couldn't find anything wrong? Huh? My family need some return on a considerable capital outlay. Three pots of lime-green puke is not enough. Are you listening, Dr Roobottom?'*

I took a deep breath, and tried to ignore the familiar roaring, fizzing feeling, which this time extended to the tips of my ears, along both arms and right down to the toenails of my little toes. But ignoring it made no difference.

'You can take that stupid grin off your face because you don't fool me. All that, "I'm such a good listener" stuff is just to cover up that it's your patients who do the work. The longer we drivel, the more you earn. What a good cover! You are totally and com-

pletely clueless. In short, you're an overqualified ninny.'

I could feel my eyes fill with tears. All these weeks and nothing had changed. Ninny? Now where on earth had that come from?

Dr Roobottom cleared his throat as Mum burst in, breathing fire — well, certainly quite thick smoke.

'What is going on in here?'

Dr Roobottom spread his hands, and looked up at her.

'It's as you see, I'm afraid. Once the patient has lost confidence in the doctor … or vice versa,' he added snakily, 'then nothing can be achieved, not anything of lasting benefit anyway.'

'What are you talking about?' I shouted in my normal voice. 'You have done absolutely nothing from start to finish.'

Mum gestured at me to be quiet. She was gazing into Robot's eyes as if he'd hypnotised her. He probably had; that would explain it.

'We mustn't waste any more of the good doctor's time, Nicky,' she murmured.

'Good doctor's time,' I echoed. 'It's rent-a-robot, for God's sake, and he's supposed to be helping me. What a joke! I doubt the moron can tie his own shoelaces.'

'Nicola,' roared Mum, 'I forbid you to say another word. You are shaming your upbringing.' I'm not kidding, those were her exact words.

Linda appeared in the doorway, a walking question mark.

'It's all right, Linda, Mrs Walters and Nicola are just leaving. They won't be needing another appointment.' Robot's expression would have made an iceberg look positively cosy.

Linda scuttled back to her desk. She gave me a friendly smile on the way out, which was not exactly what Mum was doing.

As a mark of motherly displeasure — just in case I'd suffered a total blackout of the senses and missed it — I was taken back to school for a play rehearsal that was almost over. Over the past weeks my appointments with Robot had been good for only one thing. Of course I had to attend the lunchtime rehearsals, but I had been let off the much longer one after school. Mum was well aware of how I felt about the play. It was yet another chance for Marina to rub my

nose in dirt for one thing, and how much practice do four words in Scene I and two in Scene III
need?

I was still trying to tell Mum my side of the
story when we lurched to a halt outside the
school.

'Robot was asleep for half of my appointment today. Did you know he has no idea what's
wrong with me? Actually, I don't think he's completely normal.'

'And you are, I suppose?' said Mum. It's a
wonder her tongue didn't shrivel up in all that
acid.

'Me? No, I'm a complete loser, haven't you
noticed?' She didn't hear me though; she was
busy making an unscheduled attempt to get
into the *Guinness Book of Records,* possibly in the
category of most enthusiastic tyre screecher. It
was peculiar behaviour, not at all like my
mother.

Mrs Hammond chose the play while our
drama teacher, Ms Stevenson, was away on
study leave; she decided all the parts and everything. Now it's like she expects Ms Stevenson to
do all the work. I really like Stevo, she's normally

very enthusiastic, but you can tell her heart's just not in it. She doesn't even turn up for some of the rehearsals, but who can blame her? It's a very weird play.

Having my dramatic gift reduced to a couple of insignificant words that most of the audience could easily miss when they're blowing their nose is a pain in the bum, I must say. I don't know how Mrs Hammond could have picked Marina for the lead; she's totally hopeless. I'd be *so* much better. Of course it had to be Marina I saw first as I walked into the hall, didn't it?

'Hi, Nicky. Don't you go and see a head doctor on Friday?' Marina clapped her hand over her mouth, acting like she'd said something she didn't mean to. 'Oh, sorry. I expect you're sensitive about it. I'm just surprised to see you here.'

'That's fine, Marina. It's no secret that I have a brain and you don't,' I said, smiling sweetly.

'Well at least my hands and feet work,' sneered Marina. 'It must be hard walking around with whatever's inside your head when nothing much else works either.'

Marina was not about to let me forget last Saturday. As reserve-reserve, I only played because Rochelle had the flu and Sue-Ellen accidentally flushed her sports uniform down the toilet an hour before the game. I was more than happy to donate my skirt so Sue-Ellen could play, but unfortunately Ms Woodall took the attitude that she'd proved herself unworthy of the *honour* of being in the under-13 T-ball team!

We were playing our closest rivals, which made everyone very tense. My hands always sweat when I'm nervous, and my left hand was all slippery inside a glove that was three sizes too big for me. Who has hands that big, anyway?

I dropped two catches. Well, everyone was yelling stuff, and I couldn't hear what they were shouting.

Batting was even worse. I couldn't hit the ball at all. The only thing I managed to do was knock off the rubber top to the stand so many times the umpire was itching to disqualify me. Once it went almost to first base, and would have been a good hit if it had been the ball. I wasn't allowed to run on that. Even though our team won easily, Marina totally spewed every time I did anything. In the end she tried to hide me in the outfield. Was it my fault the ball kept following me?

'You are a disgusting piece of work, Blair,' I said, quite softly.

'Well at least I *do* work, Nicky, which is more than I can say for you,' sneered Marina.

I hate to say it, but I have to thank our teacher Mrs Hammond for coming in at that moment. If she hadn't, I'd probably be up on an assault charge.

9

The next day was Saturday. I had to turn up at T-ball again but I didn't have to actually play, which gave me the chance to put in time on my tan. Nothing would make me say this out loud, but I wouldn't mind having skin like Marina's — it's no effort for her to look as if she's just returned from a cruise of the South Pacific.

The deal, apart from basking in the sun, was to take round the plate of oranges at half time, and listen to Ms Woodall tear strips off everyone because our team was trailing Perry Park by 8 runs to 3. This was one of the most enjoyable parts of the whole morning because Marina looked as if she was about to explode. She's a typical Capricorn in that respect; they're very competitive, and don't handle criticism too well. Some of the girls were in tears, which I thought was totally pathetic. I caught Sharon's eye, and we had a hard time not getting the giggles.

After half-time Perry Park began to look more like Feral Park. They were still stuck on 8 after our team took a couple of sensational catches to stop them in their tracks. Joanne began our final innings by belting the ball over the fence into Hampton Road. Kim made it to second base, even though the cow on first tried to move the plate without the umpire seeing. Marina jumped up and down and yelled 'Foul!' so loud I'm surprised a fire engine didn't arrive. A couple more of our team managed to get to first base, and, when Sharon went up to bat, the bases were loaded, which is a technical term proving that I *was* listening during the pre-game tactics session, even though Ms Woodall said I had my eyes shut! When the bases are loaded you can score four runs at once if the next batter does a big hit. Don't imagine for one second that Marina didn't let Sharon know that the welfare of the whole team, plus a couple of starving nations in Africa, depended on her.

Sharon is usually such a reliable player, but pressure does funny things to people. She kept hitting the ball into the foul zone, before eventually hitting a dolly catch straight to their left outfielder. There were howls of delight from some of Perry Park, sporting behaviour not being their main thing, and a few dirty glares for Sharon from our girls as well.

Kim made it home while the ball was in the air, so we were still in with a good chance. All we needed was one good hit to get three runs, which would make the score 8 all. Naturally Marina would spew if we only managed to draw, so I was pretty much hoping that's what would happen.

Sue-Ellen stood up to bat next, looking not so much like what the cat dragged in as something he'd totally rejected as substandard. Her parents were so cut over her sports-skirt-down-the-dunny trick that when the plumber fished it out for them they decided she had to wear it to remind her not to be so casual about her possessions. I'm not sure it'll work. For me, *casual* is not quite the word that sums up Sue-Ellen.

'What stinks?' said the grinning captain of Perry Park.

Poor Sue-Ellen turned purple. She closed her eyes, and gave a heaving shove at the ball. It sailed straight up in the air as she flung the bat down and lumbered off to first base. The other team were falling about laughing so hard that two of them collided in a heap and the ball landed just out of reach. Sue-Ellen was so relieved.

In all the confusion, Josie slid over home, and Rochelle skidded to third. The score was 8–6. Then Marina stood up, twirling the bat in the air, looking super-confident, and my whole being groaned. Here we go, another episode of 'Marina to the rescue' for the family album.

What happened next was amazing, un-believable actually, for someone living in a giant shadow. Marina smashed the ball straight at Feral Park's second base, who managed to hang onto it. Even the other team was expecting our great captain to do a saving-the-day-in-the-nick-of-time act, so they jumped around doing high fives as if they'd won the game. Marina sat down looking stunned; everyone was stunned!

There we were, still trailing by two when Rose waltzed up to the plate and casually flicked the ball all the way to the fence. This got Rochelle and Sue-Ellen home.

Rose thundered over first base and through second onto third before she even looked to see where the ball was. She took on the throw from their outfielder and sprinted for home, arriving at exactly the same moment as the ball, just managing to slide under the back-stop's arm as she reached over to tag her. We'd won 9–8, Perry Park was spewing, and I admit to screaming a few choice phrases of comparison between our two teams because my best friend Rose was the big hero on a day Marina could barely raise a smile. It doesn't get much better than that.

Most of our team walked out of the school gates together. Not Marina, though, she'd disap-peared in a puff of smoke without saying a word to anyone. The Perry Park mob were huddled around the bus stop. One girl looked over in our direction, the largest and roughest of a team not exactly bursting with young ladies. This one came complete with nose stud and chemo-style hairdo.

'What a bunch of losers! You only won because the umpire was blind.'

What did she mean? The umpire had done nothing.

'And who's the chick who smells like manure?' she went on.

'What's it to you, egghead?' I said. Several arms were trying to pull me away. Sharon hissed something, but I was listening to the noise inside my head.

'Hey, you with the big mouth. You weren't even playing, so shut yer trap.'

'But I was there, I actually saw what sort of cheats they breed at Feral Park,' I retorted weakly.

'You're dead, you stupid little tart,' said the girl, looking me straight between the eyes. What she didn't realise was that on this occasion she really should have taken it out on someone her own size, which was about twice as big as me.

'I hope you're listening, Bozo, I'm only going to say this once. You are so dumb you make Fred Flintstone look like Einstein. You wouldn't even notice if the sun went out, fell down and hit you on the conk. The only reason these other kids hang around is because they're studying single-brain-cell activity. Now get lost, and stop polluting the neighbourhood.'

I expected my friends to back me up, but when I looked at their expressions I began to feel seriously frightened, wondering if I'd escape from this latest attack complete with all my body parts.

The other Perry Park girls stood frozen to the spot. It was a bit like waiting to be struck by lightning. Then, without any warning, one of them began to laugh. Pretty soon the whole lot of them were doubled over in fits of laughter with tears streaming down their faces — it must have been mass hysteria.

The only one not laughing was the tough girl, who looked wild enough to choke. She glared at me in an 'I'll remember you' sort of way, and slouched off by herself. After a few steps she looked back at the cackling group on the footpath with a disbelieving shake of her head. I did wonder if her team would still be laughing on Monday morning.

'You were so lucky,' said Sharon. 'That was Marlene Connors. She's been suspended three times this year already.'

'Yeah,' agreed Sue-Ellen. 'I heard she brought a flick knife to school.'

So now I was insulting dangerous criminals. It had been fun in a way, having an admiring audience and a target no one felt sorry for, but I was going to land in heaps of trouble one of these days. The Robot had proved about as useful as a bag of custard, so it seemed obvious that I would have to learn to help myself. Only one problem with that brilliant theory of course — I didn't have the faintest clue where to start!

As I wandered up our street thinking these gloomy thoughts, I noticed Paul standing at our gate with a gorgeous-looking girl in her early twenties.

'Er, Nick, meet Tahnee, from Wild & Free,' he mumbled, over a pile of leaflets.

Tahnee turned to say hello, flashing a

smile full of perfect white teeth, set in a brown face framed by lots of healthy-looking hair.

'You must be Paulie's little sister, right? He's talked about you. Though *talk* is probably too strong a word; sometimes it's impossible to squeeze a word out of him. It's really nice to meet you, Nicky, and one day we must get our heads together about your little trouble.'

She nodded towards the small four-wheel drive parked on the kerb in front of our house, 'Not now though, there's lots to do.' The whole passenger side was loaded up with the same pamphlets that Paul was holding.

'Well, it sure is nice to meet you, Tahnee.' I was rather ruffled. 'Paul talks about you *all* the time,' I lied. 'We're an exceptionally close family of course, practically live in each other's pockets, so feel free to blab on about my problems to anyone you meet. Paul obviously does.'

'Don't get me wrong, not like goss or anything. Hey, this dude's practically taken a vow of silence, he barely opens his mouth, even for food. Only he wondered if anyone down the centre had heard of anything that might help, you know?'

'Well, you're experts in odd behaviour down there, I suppose, so it was worth a try, but behind this normal exterior hides ... EL FREAKO ... Yeah, that about covers it.'

I was feeling very annoyed with Paul for talking about me behind my back, but I shouldn't have taken it out on Tahnee.

She looked into my eyes. 'It's really got you down, hasn't it? Never mind, kiddo, things have a way of straightening themselves out. I've been in plenty of messes myself, so I know.'

With a cheerful wave in Paul's direction and a friendly squeeze of my shoulder, she leapt into her car, full of promises to come back one day when she wasn't so pressured.

'She seems nice,' I said.

'How could you? How could you? How ...?'

'Hey, spare me the replay in triplicate, I get the general idea. What exactly is biting you, strong, silent Paulie?'

He was so mad that I could only under-stand a fraction of what he was saying. I did gather that he thought I was the rudest person on the face of the planet, that he'd never been so humiliated in his entire life, and that he would probably never speak to me ever again! So what's new? Anyway, I was the one who should have been mad. He'd been shooting off his mouth, not me, and I must say it made a nice change.

'Tahnee? What sort of name is that? Short for Tahnee Frogmouth, I suppose?' I said to break it up. I knew this would annoy him.

'What's wrong with it?' said Paul indignantly. 'It's a New Zealand name, as a matter of fact.'

'Oh really? Doesn't that explain everything?' I can get quite sarcastic when I want to.

'What would you know, you're just a stupid little …'

Suddenly I felt tired, so I smiled sweetly up at my big brother as I came in the gate and walked up the path. 'The word I believe you are looking for Paul, is girl.'

It was his turn for a message in triplicate: 'GIRL, GIRL, GIRL.'

Then it hit me. Paul's passion to save the planet was more to do with Tahnee's natural beauty than saving a bunch of rainforests and an iceberg or two. That's why he was so cut.

10

What a great weekend! Paul sulked solidly, and refused to say another word to me. Mum was still furious about what I'd said to Robot so she didn't talk to me either, except for 'Set the table' and 'Put out the washing'. Not exactly fascinating conversation. It got quite lonely, because Dad was away playing golf at a resort down the coast. I felt quite rejected, not that anyone noticed.

By Sunday afternoon I'd started looking forward to Monday morning, and I can't remember *that* happening before. When Rose rang around four to ask if I'd like to go over for tea and to watch videos, I could tell she was surprised by my enthusiastic response.

'It's only a couple of horror movies the store was throwing out, Nick. It's not that exciting, believe me,' but I couldn't stop smiling, even after I'd put the phone down.

Waves of sound oozed from Paul's room and there was a pile of dirty crockery by his door. He was born in the wrong time zone; he should have been a caveman. Mum was reading one of her lifestyle magazines in the living room. She'd be quite happy suspending crystals and shifting our beds in line with the magnetic poles while I was out. She just grunted at me. I had no idea whether she'd heard I was going or not, but I certainly wasn't hanging round to find out.

Rose was waiting in her driveway. She was not in good shape. Our conversation was punctuated by her violent sneezes.

'Is Jeannie over?' I enquired, though I already knew. Rose nodded helplessly before sneezing three more times.

'This is going to kill me, it happens every

time Jeannie comes over,' she gasped eventually.

I decided then and there that my best friend deserved a favour, especially since she'd just rescued me from the jaws of my heartless family.

'I'll go inside and talk to her, shall I?'

Rose's eyes widened from streaming slits to about half their normal size.

'Do you think that's such a good idea?' She spluttered. 'Jeannie's great, and she gives unreal Christmas presents.'

Though I was a bit hurt, I could see her point, sort of.

'Don't worry, I never attack twice in one weekend,' I told her confidently. I *was* confident too, until I remembered the Robot incident of Friday afternoon. Along with Marlene Connors on Saturday, that made two attacks in less than a day!

Jeannie always comes over to Rose's because the rest of her family live in a small town a few hundred kilometres out west. Rose and Jeannie are second cousins, but they could be sisters except that they never fight. They're always shopping and going to movies or to the beach. They get on really well. There's only this one small problem.

It hit me the moment I opened the front door. Jeannie grew up on a pig farm actually, not that I've got anything against pigs. She's attractive, has a good figure and a great personality, but ever since she started her job as a real estate agent she's been very aware of her appearance. 'Presentation' her boss calls it, he's very hot on presentation. Unfortunately Jeannie's years on the farm had an effect on her sense of smell — killed it stone dead probably — so she doesn't seem to notice that people who get too close to her begin to choke.

'It's been such a bad year for pollen, Marjorie,' I heard her say to Rose's mum as I came into the kitchen. Mrs Stafford was hunched over the tissue box, drinking a cup of tea. They looked over and smiled a welcome. I sat down at the end of the table. Rose's mum can be a fussy old hen but she's very kind; she wouldn't want to hurt Jeannie's feelings. If anyone was going to say something it would have to be me!

'How are sales, Jeannie?' asked Mrs Stafford.

'Not too good, Marjorie, actually. The past month has been a bit of a worry. According to everyone else at the office, sales are booming, but I don't seem to shift as much as a dog kennel.'

'I've heard dogs are extremely sensitive to smell,' I threw in, trying the subtle approach. A bit too subtle actually, they both looked completely mystified.

'No, no, Nicky, that was just a figure of speech,' Jeannie explained, 'I don't actually *sell* dog kennels.' She must think I'm a total moron.

'I know you don't, Jeannie. Some people are very sensitive to smell as well, though not as sensitive as dogs, of course. Couldn't that have something to do with it?'

'I don't really see,' Jeannie was frowning a little by now, 'how *dogs* or *smells* come into it.'

I was beginning to wish I'd never started this, even before I became aware of a sort of fizzy happening. I remember thinking about that saying, 'her blood began to boil' as I ducked under the table pretending I'd dropped something. This was scary. I knew Rose would never forgive me if I opened my big mouth. Something was telling me that was just about to happen though, whether I wanted it to or not. Mrs Stafford was still talking but I didn't hear a word. I was on autopilot:

'Open those big ears of yours, Jeannie, and listen

to some good advice. Does it ever occur to you that pouring a bottle of perfume over your head is overdoing it?'

I looked at the table leg, and then slowly stuck my head up, hoping they hadn't heard. But Jeannie and Mrs Stafford had their mouths hanging open like a pair of goldfish — oh yes, they'd heard. I clamped my jaw shut, grinding my teeth together until they ached, but somehow more words escaped:

'Listen up, I'm giving you some good advice. You are not going to sell anything while you stink like the worst kind of toilet spray. And while you're at it, take a look at Rose and Marjie here. It's not hay fever — they're allergic to you.'

Actually I was feeling quite allergic to myself by this time. Rose made it even worse by coming into the room, sneezing and wheezing as badly as ever. She looked at me accusingly, out of those swollen slits that used to be eyes.

'Oh, Nicky, what have you done?'

Good question, Rose, I was just wondering that myself.

11

After Rose made up her mind never to speak to me again I should have gone straight home, but Jeannie and Mrs Stafford wouldn't hear of it.

'Leave her alone. Everyone's entitled to an opinion,' Jeannie said firmly.

I wished I hadn't made that crack about her ears; they are rather big when you look at them.

'You asked Nicky over, Rose, now be a good hostess,' said Mrs Stafford. Though I know her definition of 'good hostess' couldn't possibly include all those vicious kicks under the table and the poisonous 'how could you?' glares.

Although the food was great — as usual — it wasn't a very enjoyable meal. Afterwards Jeannie and Mrs Stafford wouldn't let me help clean up, so Rose and I watched one of the videos. Normally we'd have been laughing our heads off at the pathetic bits so it wouldn't have mattered how bad the movie was.

I said I was sorry about a thousand times, but it didn't help.

'Going already?' Mr Stafford enquired when the film was finished, looking up from the Sunday paper. 'Aren't you walking Nicky home, Rose?'

This was an old joke. I walk Rose home and she walks back with me. It can go on for hours, until we agree to stop somewhere in the middle, run home and ring each other up to see who won. When we were in Grade 3 we decided to get all technical and measure the distance between our houses, but we could never agree. Each time we paced it out we came up with something completely different. What a pair of idiots!

It felt pretty terrible to be walking down their driveway on my own.

Things hadn't improved for me at home either. Mum had moved from the living room to the kitchen, Paul was still holed up in his room, and for all I knew Dad was playing golf in the pitch dark because he still wasn't home. I decided to keep my trap shut, a novel experience, and went straight to my room without passing 'GO' or collecting $200.

After lying down and staring at nothing for about half an hour, I felt really off. I decided a shower might be just what I needed. I usually enjoy standing in the shower, watching the water slide off and the steam rise, and getting yelled at for taking all the hot water. Not tonight, though. I had a super-quick drought special, as I definitely didn't want to talk to any-one. I was feeling gross, sick and dizzy.

As I brushed my teeth and gave myself a dirty look or three in the bathroom mirror, I had the biggest shock possible. It would have given anyone a shock to have that happen. Out of my mouth came this horrible, husky, unknown voice:

'*Listen here, you moron. You're in serious dog poo. Is that how to treat your best friend? She'll never speak to you again, you know. Stop crying, you loser. No one will be impressed. Nobody cares, get it?*'

My head was hurting worse than I could believe, and that fuzzy feeling in my arms and legs that I'd first noticed at Rose's was getting worse. It was getting more and more uncomfortable every second.

I watched a stream of toothpaste bubble out of my mouth and flow down my chin before plopping onto the floor. My teeth were sort of buzzing, like they were being drilled from the inside. Someone seemed to be digging a deep hole in my stomach, using a sharp tool. Worst of all was the pain in my head. Inside this pain a horrible thought whirled round and round, it wouldn't leave me alone. You can't escape from something inside your head.

'*This is your life from now on, this is your life …*' it went. On and on. I could hardly breathe. My heart was pounding so hard I'm surprised it didn't bounce out of my chest and make a squashy sort of mess all over the bathroom floor. How much more of this could I stand? Did I have a choice?

A giant spew splattered across the bathroom. There on the floor were the remains of Mrs Stafford's delicious broccoli quiche, fresh fruit salad for dessert, and the chocolate-covered nuts and sultanas we'd eaten while pretending to watch that lame movie. Little brown nuggets, covered in bile, yuk!

I collapsed on the cold tiles. Every part of my body was doing something different and I couldn't keep up.

'Please let me die,' I groaned.

Almost immediately there was a knock on the bathroom door. Not rat-a-tat-tat, who can that be? It was more like: 'Come on out, the house is burning down!'

I lifted my head from the towel it was resting on, and sort of crab-shuffled to the door and unlocked it.

'Are you all right, Nicky?' said Mum anxiously, proving the little-known fact that all mothers can accurately locate vomit in three seconds flat, with their eyes closed and their hands tied behind their backs. 'Let me feel your forehead.'

She had me cleaned up and in bed with a glass of weak lemon cordial before I had time to blink. Best of all, she wasn't mad any more, which had to be a bonus.

As I drifted between sleeping and waking, another thought wriggled to the surface of what is laughingly called my brain. Since last Friday afternoon, a total of fifty hours or so, I had made four attacks.

Sharon would put it all down to hormones. She's been a bit boring lately, since she had this big heart-to-heart with her mother about all those really choice subjects you need to understand but don't actually want to talk about, not with your mother anyway. The two of them covered everything from body hair and female reproduction, to when your boobs grow and why you get mood swings. So now Sharon reckons we're all heading straight for these killer hormones who won't let us out of their clutches until we're too old to care.

I think she's being a bit simple. Take

Marina Blair for example, a mood swing on legs and not a boob in sight. Josie Franklin was the first girl in our grade to get her period, and she never gets too bothered about anything. I don't think hormones make all that much difference. Sharon's just showing off because she's developing quicker than Rose or me. I don't really care, I'm not too fussed about hairy armpits, if you want to know the truth.

12

I felt much better in the morning. Mum stuck her head in to see if I wanted to stay in bed. I admit to being tempted, but I'd already decided to face Rose straight away, otherwise I'd worry all day and still have to face her tomorrow. The weekend sucked, but there was no point in obsessing over it. Mum must have taken off my lucky chain when she undressed me last night because it was on my bedside table. I put it back on and jumped out of bed.

Paul had gone to an early cricket practice, which was a stroke of luck because he's a champion sulker. I was still feeling rather shaky about that auto-attack in the bathroom, and Paul picking on me was top of the list of things I could do without.

Mum was feeling very helpful. After serving a three-course breakfast she insisted on making my lunch. She even offered to drive me to school, which only happens about once a year, usually in the first week, but I wanted to see Rose as soon as possible.

Though it was almost summer you'd never have guessed. A cold wind blew ragged clouds across the place where the sun would have been if it had bothered to get up. The atmosphere at the bus stop was even chillier than the weather. It was obvious that Sharon and Rose had been talking about me, because they went all quiet. I hate that!

I said hello and tried to think of something to say, but Rose was staring at her shoes like she'd never noticed them before. In the end it was Sharon who brought up last night.

'You were out of line, Nicky, d'you know that? You should apologise.'

This took my breath away. 'Oh really? And who asked you?'

'It would be the best thing, that's all.' Sharon can be a bit smug at times. If she was a sort of human colouring-book you could take bets there'd be no smudges or scribbles over her lines. I felt like punching her in the nose — until I remembered we were friends.

'If it's any of your business, I've already said sorry. I could say it again, but it wouldn't make any difference,' I said eventually. 'Rose isn't listening.'

'You didn't have to say that stuff to Jeannie. She was offended and embarrassed, and I don't want you coming around if you can't keep your mouth shut.' Rose still wouldn't look at me. Like a volcano, it takes a lot to get her to erupt. When she does blow, you have to wait for the flow of lava to dry up, or whatever lava does. I shivered as the wind blew even harder, and I wished I'd stayed home in bed.

When the bus came, Rose and Sharon sat together in the only empty seat. I had to go down the back. The new bus driver's really strict, everyone has to have a seat; you can't sit on your bag in the aisle like we used to. It wasn't much fun seeing their two heads close together while I had to sit with a bunch of disgusting pimple brains from St Joseph's. Especially as I was certain that my former friends were still talking about me. We went to our classroom without saying any more.

Marina muttered something that sounded like 'total loser' as I brushed past on the way to my desk. I didn't knock her that hard, and I couldn't remember any special reason for her to be mad at me, so what was her problem? Normally it wouldn't have bothered me, but this morning I had this stony feeling at the bottom of my stomach.

Trust Mrs Hammond to pick on me even more than usual. It's strange, people either like you or they don't, and it doesn't have much to do with anything. We're not much different from dogs in that respect, they smell each other, and we look people up and down and kind of make up our minds. Mrs Hammond and Marina had obviously looked me up and down in exactly the same way!

At lunchtime I was on my own, which wasn't much fun. I definitely won't be encouraging

Mum to make my lunch again in a hurry. Carrot sticks are all right in their place, but ever since I made the big mistake of mentioning — just in passing — that I liked tuna sandwiches, Mum's been collecting fascinating facts about omega-3 essential fatty acids and proudly presenting them to me. I went off tuna long ago, but she'll probably be feeding me cat food for ever. And I bet no other kid gets a nutrition information chart packed inside their lunch box either.

The smell of tuna wasn't the real reason I was alone. I didn't want to eat with anyone else. They'd only ask why I wasn't sitting with Rose and Sharon. The reason for that was simple; I couldn't find them.

After lunch I felt quite sick again and very depressed. That bad thought I'd had in the bathroom seemed to have come true already. I put my head down on the desk to rest my eyes. A couple of minutes later Josie jabbed me in the back with her ruler to warn me. Too late! WHAM went Mrs Hammond's beefy mitt beside my face. It almost gave me a heart attack. I wished it had, in a way. Mum and Dad could have sued Mrs Hammond and made her pay them a lot of money if I'd died of fright. This would not only make them rich, it would be a service to humanity.

Before she could start yelling, the door opened and in walked Ms Stevenson. Even though I was so down I almost laughed when I saw the fake smile Mrs Hammond smeared over her natural snarl as she walked casually over to her desk at the front of the class.

'Can I have a word with 6B, Kaye?' said Ms Stevenson coolly. I reckon she's still cut with our teacher for making all those decisions about the play, and then nicking off and leaving Stevo to do the work. She didn't wait for an answer from Mrs Hammond either.

'Good afternoon 6B. I'm sure you all know there's only a couple of weeks to go until opening night,' she said, without waiting for an answer. 'With a little reluctance I've decided not to make the announcements from the front of stage. There'll be too much to do behind the scenes with all the costume and set changes.' Here she gave Mrs Hammond a none-too-friendly stare. Fair enough, I thought, considering she'd chosen the stupid play in the first place.

'Now, being Master of Ceremonies is a big responsibility. I've thought about it, and talked it over at length with Miss Knight. She agrees that the best person for the job is …' Mrs Hammond was looking confused, she obviously knew nothing about it.

'Nicky Walters.'

See what I mean, people either like you or they don't.

13

I had to see Ms Stevenson on Tuesday lunch-
time to talk about what she wanted me to do.
The problem, she reckoned, was that she'd done
it lots of times before and was happy to ramble
on without any prepared speech or anything,
but she was worried that someone who had
never stood up in front of a lot of people might
totally freak. I must say, when she described how
you couldn't see the audience because the lights
were shining into your eyes while they sat in the

dark watching you, that I felt fairly freaked already.

We decided on a loose sort of script in case I forgot what was about to happen. We worked on that for a while and then she asked me to start practising. Boy was she picky; 'Not too fast', 'Hurry up', 'Softer', 'Don't mumble', 'Louder', 'Stop swallowing', 'Are you breathing properly?' I never even knew there was more than one way to breathe.

Just as the bell rang, I asked, 'Why did you choose me?'

She gave me this funny little smile, and held both hands out in front, palms up, like she was helpless or something. I don't know if I was supposed to know what this meant, so I just stood there trying to look polite but interested. When it was obvious that she wasn't going to say anything, I asked straight out.

'Are you mad at Mrs Hammond for picking the play and giving out all the parts when you were away?'

'I can't discuss a fellow staff member with a student, Nicky.'

'Do you really think I'm up to this MC

thing, though? You're not just trying to annoy Mrs Hammond because she hates me, are you?'

'What on earth gave you the idea that Mrs Hammond doesn't like you?'

'It's not *that* hard to tell. She makes a disgusted face every time she looks at me.'

There was a snorting noise from Ms Stevenson as she handed me the sheets of paper with all those words I would have to say in front of hundreds of prying eyes.

'You'll be fine, Nicky. I have every confidence in you. Now run along because the bell went ages ago.'

She hustled me out of the room, and it was only as I walked into our classroom that I realised she still hadn't told me why I'd been chosen to anchor the play.

That night I felt sick again, like before. I felt gross, vomited, slept soundly, and had recovered by morning. The one difference was there was no foot-in-mouth symptoms this time, which was a relief, because I was getting quite sick of having to say sorry all the time. Mum was getting rather concerned. She wanted to take me to the doctor, but I talked her out of it. I told her it was nerves, which it could have been for all I knew.

On Wednesday nothing happened at all, and by Thursday Rose had calmed down. Jeannie had come round for tea, and when Rose told her what had been happening in my life over the last few months Jeannie not only under-stood (which was more than I did), she told Rose not to be so mean. She's very understanding, is Jeannie — even if she doesn't have any sense of smell. Rose was pretty rapt because Jeannie wanted to know if it was true about wearing too much perfume.

'Jeannie doesn't stink now and I'm not sneezing. Your big mouth's not all bad news, Nick,' finished Rose cheerfully.

'That makes a change,' I said sadly.

Sharon squeezed my arm. 'Hey, did you see Marina's face when you were picked out by Stevo? It was so good. She went bright green!'

This was comforting, and it was nice of Sharon to try to cheer me up.

'I didn't see that. I was too busy watching Mrs Hammond — she looked like she was suck-ing on a very sour lemon.'

'Everyone knows Marina only got that part because you and Ms Stevenson were away. She's hopeless. Even Rochelle reckons you'd be heaps better,' Rose said.

'It's all over the school that Stevo's so cut she threatened to walk out. And it was Miss Knight who came up with the idea of you being Master of Ceremonies. Mr Endicott was all set to do it himself, but she wouldn't let him,' added Sharon. She always knows the goss. When we're not talking I have no idea what's going on.

The next day was Friday. Ms Woodall rang before school. Joanne and Kim had chicken pox she told me, and there was no chance they'd be well enough for the match tomorrow. Great! Little Miss Stupid for trying out for the team in the first place would have to play. Worse than that, it was the Grand Final. I couldn't even look forward to getting chicken pox because I'd had it twice already.

If Rose and Sharon didn't appreciate the size of this disaster, Marina sure did. All day Friday she complained to anyone stupid enough to listen about the unfairness of it all. 'This team's worked so hard and played well all season,' she kept saying. 'For nothing.'

'We can still win,' argued Rochelle.

'No way, against St Mary's — not with the sort of dead wood we'll have to carry.' She stared straight at me as she said 'dead wood'.

'There's nothing like a positive attitude,' said Josie, trying to calm her down.

'Oh, I am positive, believe me. Positive we're going to get absolutely thrashed.'

Tara grinned at me, rolling her eyes up to the ceiling. She was the other reserve. At least she wasn't letting it get her down. Then again, Marina wasn't really talking about her or the last-minute replacement from the Grade 5 team who would come with us as a reserve. It was me she was talking about, and everyone knew it.

'Don't let it get to you. Marina's a bitch. She always has been and probably always will be,' said Sharon at lunch-time. I made the decision to appreciate all the good things about the day: I was eating lunch with my two best friends again, I wasn't eating tuna sandwiches and there wasn't a carrot stick in sight. Josie and Sue-Ellen hovered behind us.

'Do you two want to sit down?' asked Rose eventually. We'd grabbed the most sheltered spot out of a wind that felt like it was coming straight from Antarctica. They shuffled their feet in the dirt and looked embarrassed.

'No, thank you,' said Sue-Ellen, jabbing her elbow into Josie's ribcage.

'We just wanted to say we think you'll make a great announcer on play night,' said Josie. Then she took a gulp of air. 'And another thing, Nicky, don't get too nervous about tomorrow, you'll be fine.'

'Wanta bet?' I asked gloomily.

'You'll be great,' agreed Sue-Ellen, smiling at me. She looked so much nicer when she smiled.

'The world won't end if we don't win the under-13 T-ball championship anyway. Marina can get a bit obsessed. Anyway, see you around.' Josie waved.

'Yeah, bye,' added Sue-Ellen.

They walked round to the other side of the building and we looked at each other, stunned.

'Want to know the eighth wonder of the

world?' asked Sharon eventually. Rose and I nodded, still too surprised to speak.

'Marina's losing her grip. Her subjects are revolting.'

'Not as revolting as they were,' giggled Rose. 'Sue-Ellen looks almost human when she smiles.'

14

Saturday morning was worse than I expected.

Mum was dying to come, but I wouldn't let her. No way, she'd probably bond with Marina! 'What a lovely and talented girl your captain is, Nicola. What did you say her name was?' Then she'd expect me to invite her to my birthday party or something. All Friday night she was on the phone piling it on so thick you'd have thought I was about to compete in the Olympics.

'Yes, I can truthfully say that Nicky has developed a healthy interest in sport … There's nothing like playing in a team to develop self-discipline is there? … I used to be in *all* the teams when I was at school' is just a sample. I couldn't imagine who'd listen. Probably some poor sucker wanting her 'to say goodbye to house painting forever with stylish aluminium cladding in her choice of colours'. Mum loves those calls. She'll listen, but then explain in great detail why what she has is much better. I'd cross her off my list if I was a telemarketer; she'd give you a nervous breakdown.

Luckily I didn't have to convince Dad not to come to the game. He has his priorities straight, and was looking forward to sleeping in. Mum was determined though, and she'd have thought up an excuse to come. That's why I didn't tell her where we were playing.

The team met at school and caught the bus to a public oval so there'd be no home-ground advantage. When we arrived, Marina hustled us into the changing room. What was she thinking, without her we'd just sit on the bus all morning talking to the driver?

We changed and Ms Woodall jumped up and down, spat quite a lot and went red in the face for fully ten minutes. This was obviously supposed to motivate us to play well. 'I know you can do it', came up a bit, then there was the part about 'team spirit', followed by 'developing the killer instinct of a winner'. I don't know about anyone else, but her speech had a powerful effect on me. I made a legally binding agreement with myself that I would never be talked into trying out for a team ever again.

With one final 'I know you can do it', we hit the pitch.

Sharon wandered over. 'If she *knows* we can do it, why does she have to keep telling us?'

'Good question,' grinned Rose. 'Methinks she caught sight of the opposition on her way in.'

I looked over in the direction of the change rooms and gasped. 'No way! If any of those girls are under thirteen, I'm Madonna.'

Marina had seen them too — the look on her face was a classic. She could probably feel her grip on the trophy slipping already. She was so mad she was ready to chew rocks.

One look at the umpire was enough to see there'd be no help from that direction. She was about eighty-three, wore thick glasses, and obviously thought we were all here to have a jolly good time. I tucked my lucky silver chain inside my shirt for safe keeping as I waited to be sent to whatever part of the outfield Marina thought was the least likely place that anyone would hit the ball to. Looking at the size of the opposition, I knew that wherever I went the ball was sure to follow. I'd be surprised if they were *ever* under thirteen!

The first innings was a total disaster, for us, that is. Their supporters went berserk as their team smashed home run after home run. Our much smaller group of fans, mainly various relatives of Marina's, sat silently on the sidelines. There was nothing to cheer about.

Then it was our turn. Marina decided to put the good hitters at the end of the innings, which suited me. I wouldn't have to wait so long.

I didn't cover myself with glory, which was a bit monotonous. Josie managed to get to second base, but was tagged on the way to third; Sue-Ellen and Tara were caught; Sharon starred with a homer, and so did Rochelle. Rose reached second base with a good hit, but when Marina was caught by a fantastic catch in the outfield Rose was left on third base at the end of the innings.

Ms Woodall was a bit cranky with Marina about her tactics at half-time. She said that at least one perfectly good run had been thrown away with Rose left on third. Marina changed the batting order for the second innings, but what was the point? Trailing by 8–2, we didn't have much chance.

I untangled the chain round my neck and sucked an orange. It would be so good when this was over.

I actually caught someone in the second innings, one of those balls that goes up and up so far that you have time to tie your shoelaces before it lands. Marina was screaming, 'Catch it! Catch it!' What did she think I was trying to do, eat it? I ran in and stood shakily under the ball, trying not to think about all the times I'd dropped catches just like this. Then the ball dropped with a thud into my glove.

I was still shaking when Marina beckoned

me up to be back stop. Now I was supposed to catch all those balls that skew up in the air, and tag the other team before they score. It's probably the most important position in the field. Why Marina wanted me to go there was a complete mystery — it must have been sunstroke or something.

Their next batter ran to first and should have stayed there. Sharon had the ball and was hovering near second base, urging the girl to run, which she did. Sharon tagged her easily as she barged past.

Then the umpire called out that she'd been unsighted, and would give the benefit of the doubt to St Mary's. Marina's feral relatives bayed for her blood. Ms Woodall looked absolutely furious, sitting beside the other coach, who was obviously in shock herself.

I didn't really care, to tell the truth. It was so hot, and I was feeling absolutely terrible, burning up and shivering simultaneously. I opened my mouth and shut it again, and fiddled nervously with the lucky charm on my chain, but nothing could be done.

'Listen here,' I said.

The old lady turned.

'Don't think you can get away with it. I'm reporting you to the umpires' union.'

She had this sweet, understanding smile on her face, like she was going to pat me on the head and tell me not to forget we were playing a friendly game. She obviously hadn't met Marina. Besides, if it was all that friendly, why had St Mary's loaded their team with fifteen-year-olds on steroids?

'Are you listening, because I'm not going to repeat myself?'

I was speaking quietly and menacingly. Only the umpire could hear.

Then Marina, who fields at short stop, came over to argue the point, except that she didn't get a chance.

'This is corruption. We should win this game because they're cheats. The only reason for not dis-qualifying their whole team is that you're bent. And even if you can't see the nose in front of your face, that last batter was out. So what did they give you? Eh? Whatever it was, it wasn't worth it.'

The friendly smile had been replaced by a slightly dazed expression.

'This is your first and final warning. Don't mess with us. You'll be sorry if you do!'

This was the worst I'd ever felt. Watching the umpire turn a nasty shade of grey, I desperately hoped she didn't have a heart condition.

'Is that a threat?' she gasped.

'Too right,' agreed Marina enthusiastically. One of nature's bullies, our captain. 'Shall we resume playing?' she added, as we moved back to our positions.

'Batter up,' said the poor umpire, mechanically.

The rest of the match was like a dream. St Mary's had all their runs in the second innings disallowed, and they didn't all get a chance to bat.

'Three out, all out, change of innings,' chanted the ump, even though everyone is supposed to have a turn at batting in T-ball.

On the other hand nobody in our team could get out whatever they did. It didn't matter how hard St Mary's spewed. The umpire's decision is final. All the teams in the competition had to agree to that at the beginning of the season. It was totally irrelevant that the umpire was half-dead, half-blind and scared out of her wits.

We all scored runs in the second innings naturally, which meant we won the match 10–8. We were the champions!

I felt so bad on the bus that dying seemed like a good alternative. My head throbbed in time with the victory celebrations, and my stomach felt like a herd of angry toothpicks had taken up residence. Everyone singing the school song was bad enough (the singing *and* the song), but having Marina draped all over me was the total end. I couldn't believe she was happy to win the game like that. Our wonderful captain — overall sports champion of the entire school — grateful to me for fixing the umpire. Unbelievable! The only consolation was that I'd probably vomit all over her before the end of the trip.

Ms Woodall sat in front of us shaking her head. Not surprising really, considering she knows the rules. After the match she was in a huddle with the St Mary's coach for ages — something about a written protest — but the umpire was long gone, no one even saw which way she went. Rose and Sharon suspected something had happened over on home plate, but no one else had a clue. No one except Marina.

15

I took off my stupid sports skirt, rolled it into a ball and threw it on the top of my cupboard. I never wanted to see it again. Then I crawled into bed and slept for the rest of the day. Mum put this down to excitement. I decided not to tell her that I'd rather go to the dentist and have all my teeth pulled out than play in a team with Marina again.

Paul was the first person I saw, which was a surprise. He sat down on my bed and asked how I was. Sympathy is not really him, and I didn't even realise we were talking to each other again, so I was in a state of mild shock by this time.

'My head still hurts, but at least I never have to play in another team with Marina.'

'You don't look too good, actually. Shall I get Mum?'

'Just tell her I wouldn't mind something to eat,' I answered with a weak little smile. Might as well use his sympathy, before it curdled or something.

'Then you won't be down to tea?' he asked, too casually.

'What's it to you?'

'Nothing. I just wondered.' He shuffled his feet and wouldn't look at me. Something was definitely going on.

'Since when have you noticed or cared about anything, apart from how much food you can stuff in your face?'

'Who says you're sick? You're just trying to get attention,' Paul said nastily.

'I'm feeling a lot better now, as it happens, so what's happening?'

Paul was looking very uncomfortable. 'Nothing much. Only Tahnee is coming over.'

Now I was definitely getting up!

I decided that evening that I liked Tahnee a lot. She looks a bit feral, and her armpits and legs are virgin rainforest country for sure, but she has this fantastic personality. I can't imagine what she sees in Paul, though. All that silent admiration may be good for the ego but it must get a bit irritating.

Dad answered the door and was clearly blown away. Well, Tahnee's fairly stunning — men notice that sort of thing. Mum was shocked, but you could hardly tell unless you knew her. She covered it up well.

I guess what startled her most was the sort of headdress contraption that Tahnee was wearing. It was a brightly coloured band of material. Woven into the material and through her hair at the back were two small birds' nests, complete with feathers — but no eggs, I checked. She also had these cool earrings that were real bones she'd found near Uluru. Paul just stood there gawping.

I invited Tahnee to sit down and Dad

offered her a drink of something odd looking — cold-pressed apricot-kernel juice I think, which Mum had bought especially. Tahnee took one look at it and said water would be fine, or perhaps a small glass of white wine if we had any.

Pretty soon Tahnee had both Mum and Dad eating out of her hand. She told lots of stories about all the places she'd visited. It didn't seem like there was anywhere on earth left for her to go.

'She's just like Margo, isn't she, David?' asked Mum excitedly.

'Mad Margo from Moama? No, there couldn't be two of those.' Dad was grinning.

'Who are you talking about?' I asked Mum.

'My best friend at boarding school, who came from a little town on the Murray. I haven't seen her in years, but she writes to me sometimes. I wonder where she is now?'

Paul hardly said a word — even stranger, he didn't eat. Possibly he was in a coma. Tahnee didn't seem surprised; he probably always acts that way around her.

Dessert was this yummy hazelnut gâteau that passes Mum's test of good nutrition because she uses free-range eggs, brown sugar and lots of nuts.

Into a contented silence Tahnee suddenly asked how my problem was going. This was a bit too sudden for my family. We take several days to work up to a direct question like that! In fact, since that disaster of a visit to Robot, I'd said nothing to anyone.

'Oh, much the same,' I mumbled.

Tahnee turned her wide eyes on Mum. 'Wendy, I feel for your daughter,' she said. 'I went through a melancholy adolescence.' It was kind of hard to imagine her as spotty and unhappy.

'I didn't get on with my stepfather and my mother didn't back me up at all.' Tahnee was still staring at Mum. 'A good relationship with her mother is so important for a girl's self-esteem. Mine was zero when I left home.'

Mum wriggled in her seat and patted at her hair, which wasn't even untidy. She does that sometimes. 'It's lucky that Nicky and I have an excellent relationship then,' she said, without looking anywhere in particular. 'More cake anyone?'

Dad can be so embarrassing sometimes. He laughed for ages at the thought of me with low self-esteem, and then he had to mention the play. Tahnee acted like she was thrilled, and asked Paul if he'd take her. I'm 99.9% certain that my darling brother had no intention of being seen dead at my school play, but all of a sudden he was prepared to sleep out on the footpath to be sure of the best tickets!

It was strange, though, that I didn't feel like stirring Paul about Tahnee any more. It was sort of cute the way he stared at her. It's not like she's coming on to him or anything, they're just friends.

When Tahnee was going, she punched Paul on the arm, hugged me, thanked Mum for the delicious meal and told Dad that she hadn't enjoyed herself so much in ages. She must have been lying — either that or she has a very weird way of enjoying herself.

Sunday was a nothing sort of day. I lay on my bed with the notes for the play and tried not to think about what could go wrong.

In the afternoon, because I was bored, I tidied up my dresser, which hadn't closed in ages. I thought I had too many clothes. Eventually there was this huge pile by the door. Clothes I didn't like, that were too small, had stains or all three. Neatly folded in the bottom of the drawers sat three T-shirts, two jumpers and a couple of pairs of socks. How pathetic. Roll on school.

Monday assembly usually consists of Mr Endicott yelling and us trying not to listen. Occasionally Miss Knight takes it to give out awards and that sort of thing. This Monday Mr Endicott looked sulky at one end of the platform, near the stairs. Miss Knight was in the middle. We stood as the crummy recorder band played the national anthem and some horrible thing that sounded as if they made it up as they went along.

'That was very nice,' said Miss Knight. All teachers are liars, if you ask me.

Then she told us we must buy tickets for the school play. 'Don't forget the play is our major fundraiser this term, and we need to sell lots and lots of tickets. Bring the whole family along for a fun-filled evening.'

'Define "fun",' muttered Sharon.

'Marina falling over and breaking an ankle,' hissed Rose.

After that the entire T-ball team was called out. We had to stand on the platform and be presented to the school. No prizes for guessing which team member enjoyed that! The rest of us were trying to hide behind the next person so we gradually shuffled over towards the steps, near Mr Endicott, leaving Marina to collect the trophy on her own.

Miss Knight looked over to see what was going on. I wish she hadn't done that!

'One of you — Nicola, you'll do — come here and say a few words of appreciation to your captain. And the coach, Ms Woodall. Where is she? Ah, Rowena. Step up for a minute.'

Ms Woodall ran from the back of the hall, and bounded onto the stage. Sport teachers are like that — they sprint and hop and leap and jog, but never walk.

It was then that I felt this prickle down my spine and suspected something was about to happen. I just didn't realise how bad it was going to be. Marina had her arm around my shoulder like we were best pals. She announced that I had taken a fantastic catch in the final, which was rather an exaggeration in my opinion.

'Nicky is a hugely improved player since the beginning of the season, an example of what can be done with determination and hard work. Congratulations, Nicky. Well played!'

Marina is so full of crap. What she really likes is my ability to threaten old ladies.

Miss Knight smiled approvingly and passed the microphone to me. I stood with it in my hands, listening to the noise inside my head. I shut my eyes, and prayed it was a bad dream, but when I opened them nothing had changed:

'How convenient to have the whole school here so that I can tell you all exactly what I think of my number-one role model, Marina Blair.'

I felt Marina's whole body stiffen. She removed her arm from my neck, and took a couple of steps back. There was a loud gasp in the audience, which was probably Rose guessing what was about to happen. Ms Woodall was smiling encouragingly at me.

'Take your time, Nicky. Breathe deeply, there's no hurry,' said Miss Knight. Oh boy!

'*I want you all to hear this. Are you listening? Marina is without doubt* (if I'd died right then, everything would have been fine), *the most egotistical, selfish, meanest girl I have ever been unlucky enough to meet. She is prepared to lie and cheat her way to the top. If she ever gets there, spare a thought for all the people she's hurt on the way. Oh, and thanks, Ms Woodall, for coaching us. You're a great audience. Thank you all.*'

Everyone filed out in total silence, and I was led away to the principal's office.

16

I sat for about half an hour before anyone came near me.

Mum appeared, looking flustered, and we were ushered in to see the principal, Miss Knight. Mr Endicott was there too, so was Mrs Hammond and Ms Stevenson. None of them were looking too friendly and neither was Mum, so things could have been better.

'I've written a letter, Mrs Walters, about the incident at assembly. I don't want to discuss it now. I would prefer you to go home and read it with your husband and daughter, and then we'll look at the options.'

'Yes, Miss Knight.' Mum sounded like a kid, she was twisting her hands in her lap and looking upset.

'You must realise that this is a very serious infringement, Mrs Walters,' growled Mr Endicott.

'I'm aware of that. I wouldn't be here otherwise,' said Mum sharply. That was more like it.

Mrs Hammond cleared her throat and looked from Mum to me and back again. 'As Nicky won't be coming to class today, I have prepared a little work that she can do at home.' She gave Mum a thick pile of worksheets, glared at me, and excused herself.

'There is one more matter to discuss, of course. The school play.' Miss Knight paused.

'As you are aware, the first performance is scheduled for Wednesday evening. Ms Stevenson has convinced me' (though not Mr Endicott judging by his expression), 'that it is not feasible to find a replacement for Nicola at this late stage.'

There was another pause.

'I need hardly say that any repeat of this morning's incident would have very serious consequences indeed.'

That's the strange thing about Ms Knight; she's much nicer than Mr Endicott and Mrs Hammond, but when she gives you the freeze you feel so bad.

Mum didn't say much either. She dropped me at home and said she had to go out for a while, something about an interview in the paper. I seriously think she's losing her grip.

I looked through the work that I was supposed to do. Mrs Hammond is such a cow, three-quarters of the sheets were maths. Does anyone like maths? And since most of it looked like it was in Egyptian, I had no idea how to do it. I did the few sheets that involved words and then wandered around the house feeling lonely.

In the study my eye fell on the letter Miss Knight had sent. I was still reading it when Mum came home, and the weird thing is she hardly noticed. She was really odd, like she was excited or something. I suppose it's not every day that your daughter gets slung out of school.

I gave her the letter, but she barely glanced at it. I hoped Dad would be this understanding. The letter went like this:

> *Dear Mr & Mrs Walters*
>
> *With great regret I have to tell you that the behaviour of your daughter Nicola is becoming something of a problem. Her class teacher informed me some time ago of the rivalry between your daughter and another student. At the time I put this down to their different personalities. Today, however, I cannot be so lenient.*
>
> *I understand that Nicola has had a difficult few months after our earlier communication on the subject, but may I request that you seek a second opinion before this gets out of hand? It is my belief that Nicola may need medication of some kind to counteract the negativity she so obviously feels. My door is always open.*
>
> *I remain yours extremely sincerely etc, etc.*

Well, it had finally happened. My big mouth had landed me in real trouble. If I was allowed to go back to school, they'd all be watching my every little move. Marina wins again. So what's new?

When Dad came home, he and Mum had an argument. Dad said it was a waste of time to ask Robot. Finally he rang a school friend who specialises in juvenile delinquents, but Mum still planned to ring her darling Dr Roobottom. I was a little hurt by Dad's choice, I must admit, but he explained that he only wanted to find out what sort of help was available.

On Wednesday Mum went out early, and came home looking like our cat the day it ate my cousin's budgie. Well, not exactly, she didn't have feathers around her mouth, but she looked just as smug. I began to think she must be on something.

Dad dropped me at school at six o'clock that evening for one last run through before the curtain came up at eight. I hadn't eaten anything all day. I couldn't face food. Now I was feeling sick and dizzy. Everyone was really nice to me, which was a big help. They probably agreed with what I'd said in their heart of hearts. Then Marina and Mrs Hammond turned up.

'I cannot be expected to have the same dressing room,' said Marina loudly.

'There's nowhere else, dear,' said Mrs Hammond. 'Unless you want the bike shed.'

'That's not fair,' squealed Marina, stamping her foot. 'She's the one who should go.'

Ms Stevenson looked up from the button she was sewing on Sue-Ellen's cape and frowned. 'I'm in charge here,' she said icily. 'I shouldn't have to remind you that this is the Parkview school play, not Broadway. The one thing we don't need tonight is a display of artistic temperament.' That shut them both up.

By 7:15 we were all dressed and some mothers turned up to help with the makeup. I wore a plain black skirt with a white blouse, my silver chain of course, and black shoes. Pretty boring, but Ms Stevenson said it looked professional.

For the first act the whole cast had to float on as butterflies. It was so sucky. Marina was this elf creature who mended their wings. Bit of a miscast there — she'd be far more likely to pull their wings *off*.

Sharon came over to me, flapping grey and purple wings.

'Guess what?' she said. I shook my head, I was beyond guessing anything.

'Mrs Hammond's grandmother wrote the play.'

'What?'

'It's true. Josie came early and was sitting in the dressing room minding her own business when Hammy and Stevo started having this brawl on the stage. Josie thought they'd rouse on her if they found out she was listening. She crept out and made a lot of noise coming back in, and then they pretended everything was fine.'

'No wonder it's so dumb. I hate the way you never know what's going on.'

Sharon nodded. 'And if *we* don't, spare a thought for the audience.'

'But what's the point of all the different scenes?'

'Get this. Hammy told Marina to imagine she was at a banquet tasting all these courses. I have to go now and get my antennae attached. You'll kill 'em, Nick.'

Hearing the audience come in and knowing I'd soon have to stand up in front of them was the worst part. I stood in my position on the side of the stage and shook. My heart was pounding hard, while my stomach kept itself occupied doing tumble turns. It was a relief when the lights in the hall dimmed and the curtain swished open; all that waiting was really getting to me. I stepped into the spotlight and the play had begun.

It felt much better after Act I had been safely introduced. Standing in the shadows, I relaxed a bit and began to enjoy myself. Surely nothing would go wrong now.

And nothing did. Not until the very end.

In Act V we returned to the butterfly grove. Our elf (Marina) looked round as all the different characters from the whole play sort of drifted across in front of her, one by one. It didn't make any sense and was very difficult to do because of all the costume changes.

My job was to stand at the side in the dark making a 'Days of Your Life' sort of speech about the passage of time that was meant to tie up the loose ends of all the different scenes. It was Ms Stevenson's idea; Mrs Hammond hated it. I thought it was going to be fine.

'Distinguished guests, parents, teachers and friends, listen up. I apologise for making you sit through

this ridiculous play. I apologise even harder for asking you to pay to be bored out of your brain. The problem for us students is we have no rights. If a teacher says "jump", we jump. Even off a cliff, as in this case. But settle back and enjoy this last scene, secure in the knowledge that it is very short. Thank you and good-night.'

There was complete silence. I stood in the dark, crying silently.

Someone started to clap in the audience. The person stood up and shouted, 'Way to go, champ'. I realised it was Tahnee.

Then I was grabbed by the arm and pulled offstage. Mrs Hammond was fuming. I was dead meat.

Everyone had a piece of me that night. After Mrs Hammond had finished, Ms Steven-son let rip with a lot of stuff about abusing her trust and eroding her position within the staff. I'm not sure what she was on about, but it was fairly easy to see she was mad.

While all this was going on I was thinking that I'd landed myself in stacks of trouble for saying exactly the sort of things adults are always saying to us kids. No one tells them off. It's like they can be as rude as they like, and we just have to take it.

After that Miss Knight and Mr Endicott had their turn. I couldn't see how it would ever end. Just as I was thinking I'd be sitting backstage forever, getting yelled at, there was a bit of noise outside.

Tahnee burst in to rescue me. I've never been so happy to see anyone.

17

I didn't go to school on Thursday, and the excuse for cancelling the final performance of the play was that I was indisposed, but what they really meant was *uncontrolled*.

Next morning Paul told me what happened after Tahnee started to clap. Lots of people joined in. Half the audience seemed to think that what I'd said was part of the play, like a final twist or something. There were even calls through the final scene of 'Encore, encore' from the rowdiest section of the audience. It was nice of Paul to try and cheer me up.

Our local paper is delivered on Thursday afternoon. I ran out to collect it because I had nothing else to do. Much to my surprise, there was a big picture of me on the front page and a much smaller one of Mr Endicott, looking livid, even in black and white. 'DRAMATIC FINALE!' was the headline. The article underneath reviewed the play, calling it 'an uneasy attempt'. The last paragraph was the best. 'The lead in this primary school production seemed out of her depth and lacked the magnificent assurance of the Master of Ceremonies; furthermore, the script was soggy and many of the numerous scenes incomprehensible. The music, sets and costumes were excellent, however. Choice of material and faulty casting let this honest young attempt down badly.'

No special mention of the final speech, so maybe Paul was right and the audience had just accepted it as one aspect of a totally weird experience. I looked up 'incomprehensible' — it means 'cannot be understood'. Mrs Hammond will love that! Under Mr Endicott's picture the caption read, 'Herbert Endicott enjoys night out'. Somehow, I doubted it!

Miss Knight rang up a bit later. Nobody was in but me. I said I was sorry about the trouble I'd caused. She went on and on about how I'd brought the name of the school into disrepute, that I wasn't worthy to wear the uniform, and that she'd expected better of me.

Teachers all sound the same in the end, even the nice ones. You just can't trust them. 'Elbows high', they holler, as you thrash about the pool gasping for air. Believe me, the number one aim with swimming is to avoid drowning, forget the elbows. And another thing, even if you bend your knees, remember the backswing *and* keep your eye firmly on the ball, you still won't turn into the next Pat Rafter. There's obviously a secret ingredient they deliberately leave out. Deep down, all teachers hate kids. I'm sure of it.

Miss Knight stopped eventually, telling me that in her opinion my 'behaviour problems' were the result of extreme stress. Another letter to my parents was in the mail, which was something to look forward to.

It arrived next day, and said all the same

stuff over again, only more so. There was something else as well:

'*Taking everything into account, I feel it to be in the best interests of everyone to suspend Nicola from school from now until the end of term. That will provide all concerned with the necessary time and perspective to adjust to the situation.*'

The *situation*, of course, being that I was a nutcase.

Dad was cool, he thought it was a bit rough so he didn't give me a hard time, but Mum acted like I was a cockroach or some other insect pest that she'd be happy to squash under her shoe.

It was three weeks before the summer holidays started, so what on earth was I going to do? One good thing was that Mum had a new job, which meant she wouldn't be glaring at me all day. She didn't write the book I told her to, but she had sent some sample articles to several newspapers. One of them hired her to be a regular caffe latte reporter, all expenses paid. Two days a week she was to trawl the suburbs for the ultimate coffee shop, and then she was provided with a spot in front of someone's laptop so she could write her weekly article. That kept her out of my face.

I have to say that the last few months have been difficult. I've found some things out, though. For example, you can get away with anything if you do it quietly; Marina's proof of that! But if you make a noise or draw attention to yourself, you've had it. Another thing, there's definitely one rule for adults and another one for kids.

If anyone had told me at the bus stop that day I attacked the driver that I'd end up being suspended 'for bringing the name of the school into disrepute', I'd have been absolutely horrified. When it actually happened, it didn't feel that drastic a deal. After all, how bad can a nine-week holiday be? That's what Paul says anyway. It's my opinion that the *real* reason I was suspended is because no one knows what box to put me in. They haven't the slightest idea what's wrong with me.

To pass the time, since I'm sick of watching lame TV shows, I've written a list: 'Top ten reasons why Nicky Walters should be put away'.

Everyone has a different theory, except me, of course.

1. Nicky's fine, she's just going through a stage (supplied by David Walters).

2. Low self-esteem is definitely the problem (supplied by Tahnee).

3. A slow-release truth serum from the Amazon jungle is the cause (Paul's idea).

4. Acute mental and physical stress is definitely the culprit (Miss Knight's opinion).

5. This girl is a potential behaviour problem; keep future eye(s) on her! (Mr Endicott).

6. She's just a complete bitch (Marina's theory).

7. I tend to agree, darling (Mrs Hammond, who else?).

8. Hormones (Sharon has a one-track mind these days).

9. A breakdown in a gland secreting something vital for harmonic bodily function (Robot, of course, who else talks like that? Wendy Walters was the reporter).

The phone rang just as I was wondering what number 10 should be. It was Mum, and she was so excited I could almost feel the spray of saliva. The battery on her mobile was in a bad way, though.

'Wx mdx mkfj, e kkdj iw' is what it sounded like (the punctuation is mine).

'No. Still can't get it, take a deep breath and start again s-l-o-w-l-y!'

'Stop treating me like a child,' snapped Mum, suddenly clear. 'It's a little noisy here' (a slight understatement, it sounded like she was sitting on the main runway at the airport). 'Can you hear me now?' (It certainly helps when you talk in the right end). 'My best friend Margo has just come back to Australia after travelling the world and working in exotic locations. Make up the guest bedroom with flowers, clean sheets and a towel. You can do that, can't you? Make one of your lemon meringue pies, too; she'd like that.'

'Sure, Mum. Who is this Margo character anyway?'

'Don't be ridiculous. Margo's your god-mother, of course, who frequently sends you presents and cards.'

There *had* been a bizarre bark offering once, offering no clues as to its origin. No presents though, presents I would definitely remember.

'She hasn't sent me anything. I've never even heard of her.'

'Nicky, this is a little tedious. What about that silver chain you're so fond of? That was Margo, from Zanzibar if I remember rightly, where she was studying the myths and magic of Africa.'

I put down the phone and undid my lucky silver chain that I'd worn constantly over the past few months.

I felt strangely attached to it, lying there snugly in the palm of my hand. I thought and thought. Yes, I was almost certain that I'd found it underneath the paper lining of my dresser drawer the same morning I attacked Mrs Jacobs, but I had no idea where it had come from before that.

The tiny charm hanging on the chain looked like nothing really. Quite innocent! Sharon said it looked like a doughnut and that it was typical of me to be always hanging around food (she can be very droll, can Sharon). Though now I looked at a small, wide-open mouth. It was the only thing the charm could possibly be.

I turned to my list, and wrote the final item:

10. Wicked fairy godmother (Nicky's own word on the matter).

That afternoon I rode to the park on my wonky old bike. Standing by the river, I took off my lucky silver charm. This was so stupid! I shut my eyes, swung back my arm as far as it would go, and lobbed the present from my godmother into the water. It may have been my imagination, but I'm sure I heard a scream.

I whistled all the way home.